A Convenient Marriage

Ellen Rawlings

DIAMOND BOOKS, NEW YORK

This book is a Diamond original edition,
and has never been previously published.

A CONVENIENT MARRIAGE

A Diamond Book / published by arrangement with
the author

PRINTING HISTORY
Diamond edition / July 1993

ISBN: 1-55773-918-8

Diamond Books are published by The Berkley Publishing Group,
200 Madison Avenue, New York, New York 10016.
The name "DIAMOND" and its logo
are trademarks belonging to Charter Communications, Inc.

PRINTED IN THE UNITED STATES OF AMERICA

10 9 8 7 6 5 4 3 2 1

To Beth, Rebecca, David and Dave,
Justin, Ben, Darcy, and Dylan—
The Whole Tribe.

A Convenient Marriage

~Chapter 1

SEVERAL HOURS HAD passed since Mr. Roger Hammond and Mr. Severn James had begun playing cards. Most of the candles were getting low in their holders, and a few of them sputtered in a sort of last gasp before they burned out.

Mr. Hammond, in whose Grosvenor Square town house they were sitting, threw his cards on the table, then thrust back his chair. "I've had enough," he said ruefully, twisting a lock of his dark hair. "In truth, I've had more than enough. How much do I owe you, James?"

Mr. James looked at the slip of paper next to him, added its figures, then added them again. "I make it six thousand."

"Six thousand?" Mr. Hammond looked as though he were about to be sick. "I . . . I . . . You might have to wait for a bit; I don't have that much money in the house."

"That's perfectly all right," Mr. James said amicably. "Tomorrow will be soon enough."

Though possessed of a high color from too much wine, Mr. Hammond owed his flush at that moment more to worry and embarrassment than to drink. "I fear I will not be able to pay you tomorrow, either."

Mr. James crossed, then uncrossed his legs. A gentle, kindhearted man, he had no wish to distress his host. "There is no hurry," he said. "Anytime this week will do."

The problem was that Mr. Hammond could not pay his debt to Mr. James no matter what day of the week it was; nor could he pay it the following week, unless a miracle occurred. Mr. Hammond was rolled up.

He felt a moment of regret that he had not taken his daughter's advice and stopped gambling. She had begged him to, but he had been certain that his luck was in that evening and he would do very well. After all, Mr. James was known to be plump in the pocket, so that even if he were to find himself losing a few thousand or thereabout, he would not mind and would continue to play, thereby enriching Mr. Hammond. Instead it was Mr. Hammond who had lost, and badly.

Mr. Hammond started to say something, but then closed his lips and looked toward the door that led into the hall. It was opening slowly. "Oh, damn," he mumbled upon catching sight of his daughter as she entered the room.

Why he would have wanted to curse at the appearance of this glorious female, instead of singing hosannas, was a mystery to his guest, who leaped to his feet while restraining the urge to sing a few himself.

To say merely that the girl was beautiful was hardly to do her justice. In truth, she was so beautiful she made every other female he'd ever met look like dirt and ashes. Her dark hair was a luxuriant mass of curls; her brown eyes were huge and surrounded by thick lashes; her nose was small and straight; her lips deliciously pink. Her figure was outstandingly lovely, too. And she smelled of heliotrope.

Mr. James, a dedicated collector of art and exquisite *objets,* was overwhelmed. Not only was the damsel more lovely than anything in his collection but also she had the advantage of being *alive.* One could converse with her. And one could kiss and touch her—if one were very fortunate. "Behold, thou art fair, my love; behold, thou art fair," he said, substituting a quotation from the Song of Solomon for the stifled hosannas.

"It's my daughter," Mr. Hammond said unhappily.

"Gorgeous," said Mr. James, still unable to control his raptures, let along his tongue. "How old is she?"

"She's eighteen and should be making her come-out this season."

"Should be?"

"Papa," the beauty interrupted crossly, "I thought you planned to retire early tonight."

Mr. Hammond smiled uncertainly. "Did I say that? You're right; I should have done."

Mr. James cleared his throat and nudged his host. "Introduce me, please, Hammond."

"Oh, of course. Mr. James, this is my daughter, my only child, Miss Hammond."

Although Mr. James was not given to showy gestures, he bowed low, then kissed the ravishing child's hand.

She quickly pulled it back. "You should know better than to play cards with my papa," she said, more sad than accusatory. "He is not supposed to gamble."

"And who said I gambled?" her father asked indignantly.

"Didn't you?"

Instead of answering, Mr. Hammond lowered his head.

"You lost again!" Miss Hammond cried. "Oh, Papa, how could you?"

As Mr. Hammond twisted his large hands together and shifted nervously from one foot to the other, his companion stared at Mr. Hammond's daughter. He knew he was being rude, as well as making himself appear gauche, but he simply could not help himself. To look at Miss Hammond was to be sun-dazzled, star-struck, and moon-dazed.

A great longing rose in his breast. He wanted the girl for his own. True, some might think him old enough to be her father, since he was the same age as Mr. Hammond, which was thirty-eight. He was also a confirmed bachelor. But he did not wish to be a bachelor any longer. He wished to marry Miss Hammond so that she could gladden all his days—and he could gladden hers, he added in an effort to convince himself that he was being unselfish.

A faint doubt rose in him that he could indeed gladden her days, but he pushed it ruthlessly out of the way. He was determined to have her.

"Will you excuse us?" he asked her with a sweet smile. "There is something I must discuss with your papa.

Immediately afterward, I will bid him good night and he will go up to bed. Is that all right?''

Miss Hammond shrugged. ''Do you promise? Very well, then. I will see you in the morning, Papa.''

See me in the morning! Mr. James wanted to shout. See me at night, and in the afternoon, too. Love me, for I love you with all my heart.

Instead, though, he held his tongue and watched his beloved walk from the room, leaving behind the aroma of heliotrope as a gift to him. His eyes followed her until she was quite gone. Then he sighed.

''She's a hard taskmaster,'' Mr. Hammond said dolefully. ''Not like her mama in that way, rest her dear soul.''

Mr. James knew he could not rush into the proposal of marriage he planned to make. This was a delicate business. To handle it wrong would be to lose the one thing he now wanted most in all the world. He'd never forgive himself if he did that.

''An orphan, is she?'' he said in a voice filled with pity.

Mr. Hammond looked surprised. ''Why, no. That is, not exactly. She has me.''

''Ah, but who will she have when you are gone?''

''Gone?'' Mr. Hammond sounded as though the idea of his eventual demise had never entered his mind. ''Well, I don't know. I suppose she'll marry eventually, and then it will be up to her husband to care for her.''

''Yes!'' said Mr. James. Overtaken by excitement, he rose from his seat, but then forced himself to sit down again. ''Yes,'' he repeated in as serene a voice as he could manage. ''Her husband. And who will that husband be?''

Mr. Hammond shook his head. ''Damned if I know. Surely there will be someone. She's a well-looking girl.''

Well looking? Was Aphrodite merely well looking? Was Helen of Troy? ''Yes, she is,'' said Mr. James. ''And I agree. Someone will surely marry her, even though she will not have a dowry.''

Mr. Hammond looked as though he'd been bitten. ''How did you know that?''

''I surmised,'' Mr. James said carefully. ''It seems

obvious if you've been losing at cards regularly that she wouldn't have one.''

''That's true. I'm not a good papa. She deserves better.''

Here was the opening Mr. James had been waiting for. ''So she does. I could give that to her—not being her papa,'' he added hastily, ''but giving her everything a girl like her should have. I'm quite rich, you know. I have gobs and gobs of money.''

''I rather thought you did,'' Mr. Hammond said in a gloomy voice, then added, ''Are you asking me for permission to address her?''

''Yes,'' Mr. James croaked.

Mr. Hammond shook his head. ''I'm not sure about that. You're a mite old for her.''

''I thought you might say that, but don't you see? I'm just what she needs—someone older, who will take care of her and not make a fool of himself over her.''

''What? Why did you say that?''

Mr. James knew exactly why he'd said it. It was because he was sure he would make a fool of himself, was making one now. His feelings had gotten tangled up with his words. ''I didn't mean anything,'' he said. ''What is her first name?''

''Regina. My dear wife chose that name.''

''The queen,'' Mr. James murmured. ''Yes, that's fitting.''

''See here, James, you are acting rather peculiar. Are you sure you don't have something wrong with you—up here?'' He tapped his head.

Mr. James began walking in a circle. He was ruining his chances. He was his own worst enemy. ''Look,'' he said, stopping at some distance from Mr. Hammond, ''it's late, and I am tired. All I'm saying is that your daughter needs a husband who can take care of her, and I . . . I need a wife.'' Since this was the first time he had ever thought so, the words came out hesitantly.

''I'm a very, very wealthy man,'' he continued. He mentioned the sum total of his worth, and Mr. Hammond whistled. ''I can give your daughter everything she should have, and I can give you everything you should have. I will pay off all your debts, and I will cancel your debt to me. I will give your daughter a very generous settlement, and I will give you an allowance, if you'd like to have one. You'll see; it will be a convenient marriage—for all of us.''

"You do present a convincing argument," the other man said. "And it's not as though I can pay for a season for her, not now." He, too, rose and began to walk about. "The only problem is Regina."

Mr. James's eyes widened. "What do you mean?"

"She's like her mother in one way," Mr. Hammond said. "She can't really be pushed. In fact, pushing is the worst thing one can do with her. She clenches her toes and digs in, as it were."

Mr. James made a mental note of that.

"Suppose I broach the subject to her and tell her that you'll give her time to decide?" Mr. Hammond raised his hand as Mr. James began to demur. "What we need is to get the two of you away from London and all the young men here. Then she will have a chance to discover your virtues."

"Fine," said Mr. James. "Shall we go to your country home?"

Mr. Hammond reddened. "I don't have one anymore."

"Very well. We can go to mine. Shall we leave in the morning?"

"Just a minute, James. You need to calm yourself and not rush things. Probably we can leave the day after tomorrow."

"Bless you," said Mr. James. "Oh, and Hammond, consider your debt to me erased as of this minute."

Mr. Hammond beamed. "That's very generous of you, James. I'll talk to Regina as soon as I get up."

As usual, it was Regina who awoke first. She was used to rising early. Having been the mistress of the household, more or less, since her mama died four years before, she had responsibilities to which to attend, such as making certain that the maids thoroughly aired the room where her papa had played cards the evening before. First, however, she engaged in her secret morning indulgence: she turned over on her side in the high bed, closed her beautiful eyes, and daydreamed.

Her daydream was ever the same. She was married and the mistress of her own home. This was in the country and strongly resembled the family home her papa had lost at the roulette table. As always, she was seated outside in a green world of new grass, freshly leafed hedges, and budding trees. At her feet were a blue jay, an orphaned baby duck who followed her about because he thought she was his mama, and a puppy. Suddenly a shadow fell over her. Glancing up, she saw the man who was her husband. He was handsome, of course, and young, with dark hair and reckless, laughing eyes—and, it went without saying, he loved her to distraction.

Regina frowned and opened her eyes. Practically the only gentlemen she'd met thus far were middle-aged and unexciting, like the one who'd been at the house the evening before. If only her papa wouldn't keep losing at cards; then she could have a come-out with her best friend, Sally Eckle, as they'd planned. They would be sure to meet lots of young and handsome men then.

She was eating breakfast when her father entered the dining room. "Good morning," she said disapprovingly. "Are you going to bed now?"

"To bed!" Mr. Hammond said in the injured tones of the falsely accused. "I'll have you know, miss, that I've been in bed, just as I promised you last night I would do. Now I am up, ready to begin the new day." This last was said with a shudder as a beam of sunlight hit his weary-looking face. He was not used to sunlight. Ordinarily the only light that touched his face was that from candles.

"I apologize," Regina said with an affectionate smile. "Would you like some coffee?"

"No, no, what I want is some ale."

While a footman brought him his ale and he was served his breakfast, father and daughter did not speak to each other. Then Regina said, "Are you nervous about something, Papa?"

"I? Nervous? Why do you say that?"

"Your food keeps falling off your fork because your hand is shaking. Are you nervous?"

Mr. Hammond sighed. "Well, yes, a little."

"Then you must have lost last night. How much?" she asked.

Her papa put down his fork, and a saintly look appeared on his face. "Nothing," he said. "I lost absolutely nothing." Since Mr. James had canceled Mr. Hammond's debt, this statement, of course, was true.

"Oh, Papa, I'm so proud of you," Regina told him with a heartwarming smile. "Perhaps if you don't play anymore, I'll be able to have my come-out with Sally."

Mr. Hammond had forgotten that Regina hoped to share her come-out with her best friend and next-door neighbor. A shared come-out would be less expensive than one for Regina alone; but since Mr. Hammond had no money to pay for even part of one, that fact was irrelevant. He twisted his lips in a grimace, then put his dark head in his hands.

"What is it, Papa?" Regina asked in alarm. "Are you ill?"

"I have something to tell you, daughter," he said, at the same time lifting his head to glare at the servants. They vanished from the room.

"I do not have the money for a season for you. That is the way it is, and I am sorry."

"Could we not sell Mama's jewels?" Regina asked after some hesitation. "It would be for a good reason. I'm sure Mama would not mind."

"I've already sold them, and she does mind," he said, a vision of his dead wife with a frown on her beautiful face clearly before him. "There isn't a week that goes by that she doesn't come to me and say, 'Roger, I am not pleased with you. You shouldn't have sold my jewels.'"

Regina's delicate shoulders lifted. "Then there is no more to be said," she told him bravely. "I don't need a season."

"You are perfectly correct," her papa said to her surprise, "and do you know why?"

Regina shook her head.

"The reason is that you are going to become engaged shortly, to a wonderful, wealthy man who will give you heaps of jewels, and take you to France, and adore you." Mr. James had not said all of that, of course, but Mr. Hammond was sure the other man would be more than willing to do those things and anything else Regina wanted. If there was ever a besotted male, Severn James was it.

Mr. Hammond's daughter stared at him. "Who is this person, Papa? Do I know him?"

Although one could not strictly say that Regina knew Mr. James, having seen him for the first and only time the previous evening, her papa said, "Certainly you do. You can't believe I'd promise you to someone you've never even seen, can you?"

Regina looked confused, not being able to imagine who the person could be. There was the young man who had followed her and her maid home from Hatchard's Book Store more than a week ago, and still came to the house practically every day in the hope of catching a glimpse of her. Somehow, however, she could not believe that the callow young fellow was the person her father meant. There was also an older man of thirty or so who left flowers on her doorstep, and had been doing it since he saw her one evening at the ballet. Surely her papa could not think of him as being acceptable. "Who is it?" she demanded.

"I thought you'd guess it. It is the fine gentleman who was here last evening."

Regina's mouth fell open—which in no way detracted from her beauty. "You cannot mean it," she said. "He is old and not a bit like . . ." She'd been about to mention the man of her daydreams, but caught herself. She knew her papa would neither understand nor sympathize. "How could you do this to me?" she cried.

"Now, now, kitten," he said, perspiring profusely. "I haven't done anything. All I've done is agree to have us visit him at his country estate for a week . . . or two . . . or more. You still like the country, don't you?"

Indeed, she did, but not under those circumstances.

"It's so that you can get better acquainted with each other," Mr. Hammond continued in a hopeful voice. "There's no betrothal in the legal sense. I haven't signed any papers; nor has he. The truth is, if you two find after a while that you dislike each other, we will simply go home and—I don't know what we'll do. We are impoverished, Regina."

Regina leaned over and gently patted her father's arm. "Don't be upset, Papa. I don't need a season or an engagement. Indeed, I mean to obtain a position."

"A position? As what?" Mr. Hammond looked astonished.

"As . . . as a governess," Regina said haltingly, never having thought of the possibility before.

Mr. Hammond began to laugh.

"Papa, why are you doing that? Don't you believe I am well enough educated to be a governess?"

Although his laughter had stopped, Mr. Hammond chuckled for several more seconds. "Your education has nothing to do with the matter, child. It is your face. No one, and I mean no one but a blind person, is going to take a female who looks like you into her household. She'd have to be crazy. You're beautiful, Regina. And because you are, women aren't going to trust you and they aren't going to like you. They especially will not want you in their homes tempting their husbands to adultery and their sons to an unequal alliance. Besides, as James said, you deserve more than that from life. God did not give you that face and those—that figure so that you could waste them in being some vile child's governess. Let us go to James's country house, Regina. I promise you will not be sorry."

Regina gave him a considering look. "Do you think Mr. James would object if I invited Sally and her mama to accompany us?"

"Of course not," said Mr. Hammond, ready to swear to anything at this point.

"I'll think about it," Regina told him.

A few hours after this conversation was terminated, a handsome, dark-haired gentleman of about eight and twenty could have been seen staring at the Hammond town house with hard blue eyes. Dressed as he was in the height of fashion and good taste in a blue Bath coat with tails cut off just above the knees, a buff waistcoat, form-following pantaloons, and Hessians of the blackest black, he did not seem the sort one would expect to find hesitating before anyone's house, including that of the Prince Regent. "I know just how you feel," a young man in a loose Garrick addressed him. "I, too, worship at the fair Regina's feet, or would if I could manage to get near her feet."

"I beg your pardon," the gentleman replied. "Were you talking to me?"

"Of course. There's no one else here—although," he added with a sigh, "we can expect the man with the flowers to appear sooner or later. He always does."

"Do you speak English?" the gentleman asked.

The young man looked astonished. "Of course I do. That's what I am speaking now."

The handsome gentleman shifted his high-crowned beaver a bit and smoothed a lock of his dark, curly hair. "Then how is it that I cannot understand a word you are saying? I do not know who the fair Regina is, or the man with the flowers, or for that matter who you are. Would you care to explain yourself?"

The young man smiled a brave, sad smile. "I thought you were one of us," he said, "since you are hanging about Miss Hammond's house. *Us* is her admirers. There is me, and there is the man with the flowers. It was reasonable to assume that you were another among what must be a legion of the bewitched. No offense meant."

"And none taken, now that I understand you," said Steven Royce, who was the Earl of Audlin and nephew to the smitten Mr. James, who undoubtedly had earned a place for himself in the not-so-select company of idiots who made up Miss Hammond's devoted following. How his hitherto mature, stable uncle could have allowed himself to be caught by a girl of eighteen, with a father who was a notorious gambler and hadn't a feather to fly with, was more than the earl could understand. He had been stunned that morning to learn that his uncle Severn actually planned to marry the chit, and that after only seeing her once and for but a short time.

"You must have lost your wits," he'd told his uncle bluntly. "From what you've said, she has absolutely nothing in her favor and everything against her."

"It doesn't matter," Mr. James said. "I mean to marry her."

His nephew scowled. "If you must marry, surely you can find some pleasant widow who would be grateful for an agreeable husband and a nice place in which to live."

Instead of trying to convince his only relative that he was doing the right thing, Uncle Severn had stated flatly that the girl was beautiful beyond words, he was going to marry her if the king himself forbade it, and there was no more to be said. With that, he had turned his back on his nephew.

And that was why the earl was standing in front of a town house in Grosvenor Square conversing with a fool, if not a recent inmate of Bedlam.

"Good day," he said, tipping his hat, and walked up the steps to the large black door beyond which the unknown siren lurked. A haughty manner got him into the house without a question being asked.

He was led into a large, though shabby, drawing room in which light spaces on the walls proclaimed that at one time paintings had hung there. With a sneer for what they revealed about the results of Mr. Hammond's gaming habits, the Earl of Audlin seated himself and waited.

A few minutes later he was joined by Mr. Hammond. "How do you do, my lord," that gentleman said. "To what do I owe the honor of your visit?"

The earl was not one to waste words. "I am the nephew of Severn James," he said. "I have come to tell you that he must not marry your daughter."

Mr. Hammond coughed delicately. "I fear I do not understand. Did you not say that Mr. James is your uncle?" The earl nodded. "And is it not true that he is older than you?" Again, the earl nodded. "Then I do not see how you are in a position to speak for him. He is not a child."

"But he is," said the earl. "That is the point. Only a child would think he is in love after but one glimpse of a young lady."

"It was not one glimpse," Mr. Hammond corrected. "It was one meeting but a number of glimpses. Furthermore he is neither insane nor stupid, as far as I can tell. And if he wishes to marry my daughter, so be it." This was said with the force of conviction, even though Mr. Hammond well knew that his daughter did not wish to marry Mr. James.

The earl was not to be put so easily in his place, however. "He must be insane *and* stupid," he replied. "Not only is it absurd to think that he knows his own mind after one meeting with your daughter, but also it would be absurd for him to ally himself with your family."

"Just a minute . . ." said Mr. Hammond.

"I do not mean your propensity to gamble and lose," said the earl. "No, I mean that you have men, or at least a boy at the moment, hanging about your front door mooning over your daughter's feet."

Mr. Hammond raised his eyebrows. "That is hardly my fault, or my daughter's."

"You could chase him off."

"How could I? I believe he moons, as you called it, during the day. I, however, am never awake during the day, unless it is for some very special reason."

The earl's smile was cynical. "And is your reason today that you wish to discuss my uncle's proposal with your daughter?"

"That is between my daughter and me, my lord," Mr. Hammond said with dignity. "Now, if you will excuse me, I think I will return to bed. Morning air is dangerous."

The earl pulled out a large gold watch and looked at it. "It is after one o'clock," he said dryly.

"Well, no wonder I feel as I do," said Mr. Hammond, rubbing a hand limply over his eyes. "I bid you good day, my lord."

The Earl of Audlin was not used to being dismissed. "Just one moment," he said sharply, but then stopped speaking. The most intoxicating creature he'd ever seen had just walked into the room. Without taking his eyes off of her, he stood.

The intoxicating creature, of course, was Regina. She was wearing a simple blue muslin dress that clung lovingly to her high breasts and tiny waist. Her dark hair, unbound except for a snood, was in delightful little wisps and ringlets about her face. And her face—that face . . . The earl gulped.

Regina did so as well. As incredible as it might seem, here, before her, was the man of her daydreams. Her face aglow, she gave him a dazzling smile.

For a moment the earl could not remember why he had come there. He almost smiled back, but caught himself in time. The little hussy; she was trying to entangle him in her net, too.

It was not surprising to him, now that he'd seen her, that his uncle had been carried away by her. It would take a more stalwart person than Severn James to withstand such beauty. It would take a person like the Earl of Audlin!

"Are you Miss Hammond?" he asked in a cold voice.

The man of Regina's dreams would never speak to her in such an off-putting tone. She gave him a puzzled look and nodded.

"And do you think you are engaged to my uncle?"

The dream shattered. This was no hero; this was a person who did not like her. Although she was not especially used to adoration, having just outgrown her puppy fat, she knew that lately men tended to admire her appearance and to be very kind to her. After the butcher had seen her only one time, he always supplied the family with the very best lamb and mutton. The fishmonger had responded in the same way. Yet here was this stranger speaking to her in a voice that intimated that she was a blot upon the escutcheon of mankind.

"Who are you?" she asked.

"I am Audlin."

She could be cold, too. "Well?"

The earl was not used to being treated dismissively. After

all, he was titled, wealthy, not unattractive, and still unmarried. He was quite a prize, all things considered.

This beauty obviously did not think so, however. How dare she! The earl's blue eyes narrowed, his thin nostrils flared, and his stubborn chin went out. Despite herself, Regina gave a little shiver.

The earl noticed it and sprang. "I am glad you recognize that I am not to be trifled with," he said with more satisfaction than the situation seemed to warrant. "Now, simply promise me that you will not accept my uncle's offer of marriage, and I will leave."

"Never," said the scorned young woman.

"Never?" the earl repeated.

"You heard me."

The earl reseated himself without asking permission and stretched out his long limbs. Regina flushed at the implied insult. "Get up," she said, "and go away. I do not wish to speak with you, nor does my father."

"I shall leave as soon as you give me your word."

"Shall you? No, you shan't. This is our house, my lord."

"Are you certain that it still is?" the earl asked, thinking of her papa's gambling propensities. The implication was not lost upon Regina. She looked at him with contempt—a contempt even he believed he deserved. "I am sorry I said that," he said quietly. "I should not have."

If he thought his apology would mollify her, he was wrong. "You are a despicable man," she said, "and I do not accept your apology."

He had feared she might burst into tears; and though he would have felt ashamed that he was the cause of the waterworks, he would have understood Regina's reaction. Young girls were supposed to cry when they were in a difficult situation; they were not supposed to remain dry-eyed and on the offensive. Steven felt a grudging admiration for her.

Nevertheless he still did not agree that his uncle should marry her. He was convinced that Miss Hammond was not his uncle's type and would bring nothing but misery to the man. Even a besotted person, which his uncle undoubtedly was, eventually got over his passion, especially when all that nurtured it was a young woman's ephemeral good looks.

"You seem like a sensible girl," he said to Regina. "Confess it—you don't really want to marry a man as old as your own papa, do you?"

"Just a moment . . ." said Mr. Hammond. Regina, however, merely tightened her beautiful lips and stared at him.

Why did he have this mad desire to kiss those lips? He must be as much of a fool as his uncle.

But he would not be. No silly young thing was going to make him lose his wits, no matter how ravishing she was.

He just needed to be a bit diplomatic in order to get his way. "I've heard you've had some reverses," he said more mildly. "I do understand. How much can I give you?"

Regina stared at him in puzzlement. "How much of what?"

He frowned at her as though she were being deliberately obtuse. "How much money will it take for you not to need my uncle's money?"

"Now, see here, Audlin," Mr. Hammond said, "don't make me have to call you out."

"Call him out, Papa," the suddenly savage young beauty said. "Call him out and shoot him right between his eyes. If you don't, I will."

"You see what you've done, Audlin," Mr. Hammond said angrily. "You've caused my daughter to lose all control of herself. You ought to be ashamed."

The earl flushed. "I . . . There is just something about you, Miss Hammond, which makes me lose control of myself as well—of my temper, that is."

Yes, and he knew what it was. It was unnerving for a man to have to fight his inclinations, especially when they were so against his principles. He didn't want to argue with Miss Hammond. He wanted to take her into his arms and kiss her until she was dizzy. Then he wanted to—never mind that.

All of a sudden he felt sorry for his uncle.

He directed himself to Mr. Hammond. "My uncle says

that he has invited you and your daughter to Fairways, his estate in Kent.''

Mr. Hammond nodded stiffly.

''I want to add my voice to that invitation.''

''Is that necessary?'' Miss Hammond said, sounding belligerent. ''It isn't your estate, after all.''

The earl was now all patience and sweet reasonableness. ''No, it is not. What I meant was that I withdraw my objection to your visit, if not to your engagement. Tell me, Miss Hammond, do you truly want to be engaged to my uncle? He is very staid. With all due respect to my uncle, I do not think you would enjoy being married to him.''

Regina didn't think so, either. ''I would love being married to him,'' she said. ''In truth, I cannot wait.''

''Why, Regina,'' said her papa, ''that is not the impression you gave me. Just a few hours ago you were asking me how I could do such a thing as to promise you to Mr. James. What has caused you to change your mind?''

Regina's exquisite face registered disgust at her father's artlessness.

''Did I say something wrong?'' Mr. Hammond asked.

''No, you said exactly the right thing,'' answered the earl, an upwelling of pleasurable excitement making him raise his voice. ''I knew she didn't want him. I knew it.''

''Even if I don't, I mean to marry him,'' Regina said. She sounded implacable. ''I will marry him if it's the last thing I do, and neither you nor anyone else will stop me. And after I do, my lord, be assured that you will not be welcome at any of our houses.''

There! That would teach him to destroy her illusions.

~Chapter 2

LORD AUDLIN ENTERED his uncle's town house in Berkeley Square and turned toward the library, even before the butler told him his uncle was there. Severn James was almost always in his library, because, except for an occasional game of cards, and now Miss Hammond, reading was his great passion.

Even if it had not been, the earl would have understood why the room held such appeal for him. It was furnished with deep, comfortable seating pieces; its two fireplaces, neither in use this day, sported bargello fire screens that family legend said had been made by Mary, Queen of Scots; and its pale blue walls were filled with handsome mahogany bookcases whose glass doors revealed richly leatherbound tomes. In addition, there was a generous representation of the paintings and sculpture his uncle so lovingly collected.

Mr. James was ensconced in a high-backed burgundy chair, his feet upon a hassock, reading Euripides' *Alcestis* in the original Greek. Apparently deep into the tragedy, he barely looked up when his nephew walked in.

"I saw your princess yesterday afternoon," Lord Audlin said while seating himself near his uncle.

Mr. James slapped down his book. His face lit up. "Did you really? Where?"

"At her house," the earl said matter-of-factly. "I went to call upon her and her father in Grosvenor Square."

The elation upon Mr. James's pleasant face was replaced by a worried look. "I hope you didn't say anything to her

19

that you shouldn't have. I would be seriously displeased, Steven, if you did."

"You can be assured that everything I said was exactly what I should have," the earl replied with a sardonic smile.

"Good, good," his uncle told him happily, obviously missing the import of the smile. "For a moment I was afraid that you'd gone to ring a peal over Miss Hammond's head and that of her father, because you did not seem at all pleased when I told you I meant to become engaged to her."

He passed a slightly trembling hand over his forehead. "She has agreed to become engaged to me, hasn't she? Her father was not certain that she would care to be."

The earl leaned back in his chair and extended his long, booted legs. "My impression is that you are engaged to become engaged, after a mutual sojourn of a week or so at Fairways."

"Yes, that is exactly what I hoped. So, you liked her. I am glad. I must confess that I feared you would not. You do sometimes take an odd, inexplicable dislike to certain people."

The earl raised a dark eyebrow. "And you, my dear uncle, never do—but sometimes should." He wanted to say more, much of it to the effect that it wasn't he who was making a blasted fool of himself over a girl who was not yet out. He had decided after his meeting with Regina, however, that he would not achieve his goal by separating his uncle from the luscious object of his obsession by using insults. No, the way to get him to relinquish the fair Regina—for his own good, naturally—was to make him come to the realization that he and she were wrong for each other. How the earl would accomplish this end he had not fully worked out yet, but do it he would. The expression on his good-looking face hardened as he thought about the delicate, but necessary, business facing him.

As for Miss Hammond, it had surprised him that she was so adamant about becoming betrothed to his uncle. Of course, her reasons had to be avaricious; but in that case, she was making a mistake. There were richer men in the ton than his uncle—like the earl himself—and younger, too—

again like him. Not that the glorious Miss Hammond could have had a hope of ensnaring him in her web. He could not remember disapproving of any female more.

"She seemed delighted at the idea of becoming affianced to you," he said, which, in a sense, was no more than the truth.

Mr. James stroked his blond hair, then threaded his fingers together and tapped his toes. It was as though he were bursting with excitement but did not know how to express it properly. "Did she? Hallelujah!" he cried.

His uncle was worse off than the earl had realized. Hallelujah, indeed! "I have decided to go to Fairways with you," he said, "to help you entertain your fiancée and her papa—that is, if it is all right with you."

Mr. James beamed at him. "You are very welcome. Indeed, I couldn't be more pleased," he said sincerely.

The earl's own smile was cool. "I know how the unfledged chicks are. They've seen so little and done so little that it is a real chore for a grown-up to find something to talk about with them. I don't want you to have to go through the ordeal by yourself."

His uncle's face fell. "Oh, do you think so? I suppose you'd know better than I. In any case, that is very kind of you."

For just a minute the earl's resolve wavered. His uncle was such a nice person, so decent and trusting, that he hated to deal in an underhanded way with him. But wasn't the man's niceness the reason Steven had to save him from making the greatest mistake of his life? It wouldn't be easy, given the attractions of the vixen, but someone had to do it.

"Tell me," Uncle Severn asked, "what did you think of her? Is she not divine?"

Divine was hardly the word Steven would have chosen, not when it came to describing Miss Hammond's character. "Yes, she is," he said in a flat, unemotional tone.

His uncle stared at him. "I do not see how you can say that so prosaically. Don't you think she is the most beautiful young woman you have ever seen?"

"As to that," Steven replied as though he were seriously

considering the matter, "I am not certain. I've seen so many beautiful women, you know. Just last week I saw a tall young woman with green eyes who was—"

His uncle would not let him finish. "She couldn't have been more lovely than Regina. Have you ever seen a more glorious head of hair than hers?"

Feeling that he had distressed his uncle as much as he could without giving away his game, the earl admitted that he had not. He then went on to agree that Regina had the most beautiful eyes, ears, nose, and chin, not to mention other parts, he had ever seen.

It was not easy for him to do this, of course, given his feelings; nevertheless he would go to greater lengths, if necessary, to save his uncle from such a disastrous alliance. The important thing was not to be obvious; his uncle would be put right off by an overt attack on his lady love. No, as much as he wanted to, Steven would not do that. He would go to Fairways with his uncle and Miss Hammond, and her papa, of course, and work his wiles there. He had no doubt that in two weeks at the limit he would have convinced his uncle that Regina Hammond was utterly wrong for him. However, just in case something went awry and his plan failed, he would convince her that his uncle was utterly wrong for her. And if that was not successful, he would make the supreme sacrifice and use himself—and his money—as the bait to draw the young lady into showing her true colors. He had never felt so determined. He could not fail.

A few days later the whole party set off for Fairways, Mr. James's country home in Kent. Regina, her papa, and Mr. James crowded into one carriage along with Sally Eckle, a red-haired, freckle-faced colt of a girl, and Mrs. Eckle. Regina had continued to insist that she could not go upon a visit without Sally. Sally's mother, an overprotective widow, had insisted that Sally could not go upon a visit without her mama. The earl's love-bitten uncle had agreed, of course, to the addition of these two people to their group. He would have agreed to the addition of the entire Royal

Horse Guard, black helmets, blue jackets, horses, and all, if that had been what Regina requested.

The earl rode his roan gelding alongside their carriage. Regina felt disappointed at first at his not sitting inside the carriage with them; although unpleasant, he was at least comparatively young. On second thought, however, she decided it was better that they keep their distance from each other. She still resented the fact that "the man of her daydreams" had turned out to be more suitable for a role in a nightmare.

"I'm so glad the earl isn't riding in the coach," she whispered to Sally. "Aren't you?"

Her friend sighed. "I suppose his absence does make it easier for me."

Regina stared at her blankly. "Easier? What do you mean?"

"Something momentous has happened," Regina's friend whispered.

"Girls, don't whisper; it's rude," said Mrs. Eckle, cutting off the exchange.

Regina had to wait until they stopped for a luncheon before she could become enlightened. Enlightenment came in the form of a note. *Dear Regina,* the note from Sally said, *I am in love. The one I love is the earl. Do you think I can make him love me? Your friend, Sally.*

"Take this," she hissed as Regina was about to go up the steps again into the carriage. "Don't breathe a word."

Regina turned her back to the others to read the note. "Oh, no," she said before slipping it into her blue reticule. The whole rest of the trip to Fairways, whenever she thought of the contents of the note, she stared accusingly at Sally as though the latter had betrayed her country to its vilest enemies.

At last they came to a handsome wrought-iron fence embellished every few yards with small, gilded griffins. In the center of the area was a stone gatehouse. "We are here," Mr. James announced joyously. "Fairways for the fair."

Regina raised an eyebrow, and her lips thinned. Sally,

however, presumably because she, too, felt the pangs of love, gave him a pitying look.

The house was a huge, sprawling affair, built for the most part of red brick, although some of the older parts were constructed of stone. The front of the house boasted six white columns, and the walnut-colored entry doors had a single column on each side, like a sentry standing at attention. The edifice stood in a pretty park. "Mr. James must be very rich," Sally whispered to Regina, before her mother poked her in the ribs with an elbow.

Soon everyone was settled in, with the two girls, at their request, sharing a room. "Isn't this divine?" Sally said, whirling around on the cream-and-red Savonnerie rug before collapsing bonelessly onto a huge four-poster hung with pink-and-cream-colored curtains.

Regina frowned. She had felt out of sorts since she'd received Sally's message. How could her friend have conceived a tendre for a ruthless savage like Lord Audlin? It was Regina's duty to see that Sally's feelings for the evil earl died aborning.

"Sally, I have something important to talk about with you," she said.

"And I have something important to talk about with you," her friend replied.

"I hope it is not about the earl," Regina said crossly.

"No, it isn't precisely. Shall I go first?"

Regina pulled a red velvet chair over to the bed and sat down, folding her small hands primly in her lap. "Very well. What is it?"

"My mama didn't want us to come on this visit with you," Sally stated baldly.

Regina's large brown eyes took on a look of distress. "Why ever not?"

"She said—oh, Regina, she said that you are beautiful, and I, though well enough, am not, and that beside you I am unnoticeable; she said even she doesn't notice me when I am with you, and she is my mama who loves me. She said that to men, I will be invisible, and since it is men I should be thinking about now, it is not good for me to be too much in your company.''

Regina was deeply hurt. "We've been friends forever, Sally. How could she be like that?" Sally shook her head.

"Do you remember," Regina asked, "when you called me a bad name when we were four, and your mama made your nurse wash out your mouth with laundry soap?"

Sally giggled. "Yes, and do you remember when we were seven and you threw a scone at me when you discovered I'd cut your dolly's hair?"

"Of course I do. I just don't understand your mama, especially because what she said can't be true."

Sally looked interested. "Really? Why can't it?"

"Because *you* are beautiful."

Sally stared at her friend, who looked back at her steadfastly, obviously sincere about what she had just said. Sally started to laugh, then leaned over and hugged her. "Oh, Regina, you are my dearest, dearest friend, and I will disobey my mama and do anything for you—except stop loving the earl."

At once Regina grew stern. "It is about the earl that I want to talk to you. Could you explain to me why you feel you are in love with him? You do not even know him."

"That is easy to answer. The first time I looked at him, outside of your house, I could hardly catch my breath. My heart raced. My palms got wet. I knew if he touched me, I'd die. It's been that way ever since."

"Ever since?" Regina asked, conveniently forgetting that her heart had raced as well the first time she'd glimpsed Lord Audlin—before she'd learned what a miserable person he was. "Do you mean while he was riding beside our coach and when you sat across from him at the inn?"

Sally nodded, causing Regina to shake her head in puzzlement. "But why do you feel that way about him? He is not a very nice person."

"As though I'd care about that," her friend said scornfully. He is beautiful! Can a man be beautiful? Never mind. Just think of his hair. Did you see how it curls? I'll wager it does that by itself, not because his valet fixes it. And his eyes, they are as blue as . . . as blue as . . . something very blue. He is my soul mate—I recognized that instantly—and I'd do anything for him.''

"You said you'd do anything for me."

"That is different. He is my beloved, not my friend, so anything he commanded I would have to do without even thinking about it. *Anything!*"

Regina was aghast. More sharply than she meant, she said, "You must not talk like that, Sally. The earl is almost certainly a rake and a libertine. He would flirt with you and kiss you; then he would cast you aside."

"Oh, do you think so?" Sally asked hopefully. "I mean the first two parts of what you said?"

Regina never should have insisted upon having Sally included in their visit. It was her fault that this dreadful attraction had taken place. The earl was utterly wrong for Sally, and Regina must convince her of that fact. However, just in case she failed, she would have to convince the earl that Sally was not for him. And if that was not successful, as distasteful as it would be, she would make the supreme sacrifice and use herself as the bait to draw the earl into showing his true colors. Regina had never felt so adamant about anything before in her life. She could not fail.

The earl, proceeding according to his own agenda, saw to it that his uncle and the two young ladies were awakened early the next day. Although the girls did not mind, indeed, had been awake a half hour or more before he had them roused, his uncle did mind. "It is the middle of the night," he said, grumbling.

The earl laughed. "It's hardly that. Besides, don't you want to keep Miss Hammond and Miss Eckle amused? You know how young girls are. If they don't have something to do every minute, they get bored and either launch themselves into trouble or lapse into melancholia—or ask to be taken back to London right away. You wouldn't want them to leave the day after they got here, would you?"

Severn James leaped out of bed and tore off his nightcap.

"No, certainly not," he said. "Tell them to expect me downstairs in twenty minutes. Make that ten."

Smiling, the earl nodded. A few more early mornings like this one, he thought, and his uncle would probably be delighted to rid himself of the youthful Miss Hammond.

When his uncle joined them at the breakfast table, no ill effects were apparent in him. The earl would have to try harder. And what better way to show his uncle that it was inappropriate for him to court an eighteen-year-old, even a very beautiful one, than to keep him occupied at strenuous athletic activities? "Let us not dawdle," he said. "It is a fine day, and we'll not want to miss a minute of being outdoors and riding. I have had the grooms already bring the horses around."

Mr. James peered out the window. "It's misting," he said, "and appears to be cold."

"That shouldn't stop us," the earl declared. "Should it, Miss Hammond?" Although Regina declined to answer, Miss Eckle agreed heartily that it should not.

For the girls, the exercise was no hardship. "I love to ride," declared Miss Eckle as they went down a path on Mr. James's estate. She beamed into the earl's face. "How clever of you to have thought of that."

Regina gave him a sour smile.

Mr. James, however, was a different case. "Do you think we could ride a little more slowly?" he asked his nephew plaintively, after they had been out close to an hour. "Miss Hammond and Miss Eckle must be getting exhausted."

"Oh, no," both of them called from their mounts.

Sally gave her mare a pat. "I could do this forever," she said enthusiastically.

"So could I," Regina agreed despite her desire not to approve of anything the earl suggested.

Mr. James smiled weakly and did not make another such request.

The next thing the earl had them do, directly after a late lunch, was to take a long walk. Although the weather was now warm and dry, Mr. James was not eager to go for a walk. He protested that he needed to attend to other matters, such as visits to some of his tenants. However, the earl convinced him that it was his duty, at least the first full day of his guests' visit, to entertain them. "Besides," he said ominously, "remember what I told you about young ladies who become bored."

Not having any acquaintance with young women, Mr. James had no idea how they became, bored or not; the earl could have told him anything. Of one fact he was certain, however: he could not bear to cause his dear Miss Hammond to experience even a moment of unhappiness. If walking was what she needed, walk they would.

The place the earl chose for them to start their walk was at the bottom of a high, grass-covered hill. "How beautiful," Regina said, looking around. "Just a moment, if you please." From the pocket of her skirt she took a little sack, the contents of which she shook into her hand. Then she whistled.

In no time at all, a robin flew up to her and alit on her hand. Bending his olive-brown head, he took some of the food from her.

Regina put her face quite close to his red breast, a seraphic smile on her lips. The robin brushed his little body against her cheek and sat there as though enjoying the contact as much as she. The next minute he flew off.

"I've never seen anything like it," Mr. James said, looking at Regina as though she were the Church of England's answer to St. Francis, and he should be on his knees, adoring her.

"Regina always does that," Sally advised. "All animals love her, especially birds."

Regina glanced over at the earl. There was a strange look on his face. If it were not utterly ridiculous, she'd think he was jealous. Jealous of a bird? How excessively odd. And why be jealous at all when he disliked her so? No, she thought, she must have imagined the look, or mistaken the cause. When she turned back, his habitual expression when he perceived her was on his face: a combination of dislike and disdain.

"It shouldn't take us long to get to the top," the earl said grimly. "I hope you put on stout walking shoes, Miss Eckle."

"I did," Sally said agreeably, giving them a glimpse of a pale blue leather half boot.

"Yes," said Regina, doing the same.

The earl peered downward in the hope that he might see a bit of her ankle and leg. He had no doubt that both were quite beautiful. As though to thwart him, Regina tugged at her linen skirt so that nothing but the tips of her brown boots showed.

Mr. James peered doubtfully at his own boots. Though polished to a fare-thee-well, they did not seem as if they were meant for hiking. "I don't know. . . ." he said.

"Oh, come along," Sally told him, with a tug at his arm. "We'll help you if you start to slide; won't we, Regina?"

As Regina nodded her head Mr. James blushed. "I wouldn't want to hold you up," he said. "I'm afraid I'm more used to sitting and reading Homer than climbing hills."

"I've read Homer," Sally told him enthusiastically. She gave him a big smile. I read the *Aenead,* in English; I don't read Greek."

"Did you?" Mr. James said, staring at Regina. "That's wonderful."

"I think Homer wrote the *Aenead* in Latin," Regina pointed out in a low voice.

Sally flushed, as did Regina, who said, "I'm sorry."

"It is perfectly understandable that both of you should believe as you do," Mr. James announced. "Although the scholars I've read don't think that Homer wrote the *Aenead,* a few might."

The earl was astonished. If anyone should—and did—know that it was Virgil who was the author of the *Aenead,* it was his bookish uncle. Would the man go to any lengths to protect these females, even to the point of intellectual dishonesty? The earl was truly worried now.

"Come, Miss Hammond," Mr. James said tenderly. He went to the head of their little group and set off up the hill.

Eventually they reached the top. "Whew," said Sally,

tugging off her chip straw bonnet so that she could fan
herself with it. "That was difficult."

"It was fun," Regina said, leaving her bonnet alone,
probably because she did not seem to have perspired even a
little but still looked cool, clean, and exquisite.

Mr. James was leaning against a tree, either with nothing
to say or having lost the strength to say it. His face was very
red.

The earl, seeming as untaxed as Regina, smiled wickedly
at them. "Shall we go back down now?" he said, standing
on the edge of the incline, his hands on his lean hips and his
feet planted wide as if he had just conquered some brave
new world.

The next moment he apparently lost his balance.
"Whoa," said the earl. He grabbed hold of Regina, and the
two of them went rolling down the hill.

"Miss Hammond, oh, Miss Hammond," called Mr.
James, in obvious distress. As fast as he could, he slid down
the path to reach his poor dearest darling. Miss Eckle came
right behind him.

As might be expected, Regina and the earl reached the
bottom before the others. The two of them lay next to each
other, sprawled on their backs, their arms flung wide.
Regina realized that one of her hands was touching the
earl's hard chest. She couldn't have pulled it away any
faster if that part of his anatomy had been on fire.

"You pushed me, didn't you?" the earl said, twisting his
head toward her.

Regina grinned. "I, my lord? Why would I want to do
that? It's not as though I would have a reason to wish to
punish you."

Lord Audlin turned over lazily, bent his elbow, and
propped his handsome head on his hand. His face was right
above hers. "Your hat is squashed," he said, looking down
at her. He was very close.

"Is it?" Regina asked weakly. She shut her eyes.

"What long, thick lashes you have," the earl said
wonderingly.

Her eyes opened a fraction. "So do you."

"Do I? I've never noticed."

Regina had noticed, all right. That was one reason why she had shut her eyes in the first place. Staring at his dark lashes and looking into his blue eyes made her exceedingly . . . um, nervous.

"Does anything hurt?" he asked.

She twitched her shoulders and moved her limbs, once more with her eyes shut tight. "No. Does anything hurt on you?"

"No. Did you have fun rolling down the hill?"

Regina sat up quickly, almost bumping into his face. "Fun?" she asked. "Rolling down a hill?" She felt her hat and, finding that it was indeed squashed, pulled it off. The sun painted her dark hair with loving splashes of gold.

She looked to the top of the hill, then over at the earl. "Yes," she said with a reluctant grin, "I did. It was exciting."

"Yes, you are," the earl replied before he could stop himself.

He gave her a furtive look. Blast! Had she heard him? How could she not have?

Huffing and puffing, Mr. James finally reached them. "Are you all right, my *dear* Miss Hammond?" he gasped.

"I am fine," she said serenely, making the earl think that she must not have heard him. He'd have to watch himself, he thought with a frown. Otherwise, like his uncle, he would fall under the witch's spell. He had no intention of doing that.

"Tell me you are all right." This was Miss Eckle, addressing Lord Audlin. He started to smile politely, then took a good look at her face. Her freckles stood out vividly on her skin, and she seemed about to cry. Good God! Was it possible?

"I am fine," he said.

She gave him a tender smile. "I am so glad." Unconsciously she patted his hand. "If anything had happened to you . . ."

It was more than possible. It seemed incontrovertible. While he'd been trying to cure his love-struck uncle of being under Miss Hammond's spell, Miss Eckle had been falling in love with him as fast as she could. Suddenly the earl felt weary. What a coil.

He would have to think about Miss Eckle's problem later, he decided. He was still at work on the present one of his uncle's infatuation with Miss Hammond.

Now, he had another exercise for them. If that didn't convince his uncle that he was too old for Miss Hammond, probably nothing would.

"We're going to have an archery contest," he announced. "Won't that be grand?"

"Archery?" Mr. James echoed in a tone of dismay. "I haven't used a bow and arrow since I was . . . since I was—I was a bit younger the last time I did."

"You'll be splendid," Sally told him, after waiting in vain for the silent Regina to offer him reassurances. "And you have marvelous ideas, my lord," she added, looking up at the earl with love-dazzled eyes.

He definitely would have to do something about that girl.

Miss Eckle had the honor of shooting first. Her initial arrow went close to the mark. Her second and third, however, fell in the dirt because at the critical moment each time she turned to look at Lord Audlin.

Mr. James went next. "Oops," he said as his arrow fell from the bow. He bent to pick it up. "There's no problem," he said. "It will all come back to me in a minute or two."

This time his arrow went off. However, it missed the target and landed somewhere in the grass. "I'm sorry about that," he said. His pale skin turned red from exertion and embarrassment.

"That's too bad," Sally said gently; she still felt pity for him having had the bad luck to fall in love with Regina. Not only that, but he had obviously been exhausted by their ride and walk. He was not faring well. "You'll do better next time," she said kindly.

"Do you think so?" He gave her a grateful smile.

Sally's kind heart was touched. "Here, let me help you look for your arrow."

Regina, of course, didn't care if Mr. James hit or missed

his target or stopped playing altogether. Her goal was to defeat the earl. Fortunately she had a good eye and a steady hand. Two of her arrows hit quite close to the bull's-eye. The last pierced it dead center.

"You're a formidable opponent," said the earl, stepping forward.

Suddenly, for the first time, Regina really looked at him and saw him, not as the personification of the man in her daydreams but as a real, flesh-and-blood person. My, he was handsome, she thought, watching him stand bareheaded; a gentle breeze played with the black curls at his temple.

"I wish I could touch his hair," Sally whispered. "See how dark it is, like a . . . like a . . . like something very dark."

Regina noticed how the muscles in his arms flexed as he pulled back on the bow. His arrow flew across the intervening space and hit right next to hers in the bull's-eye. He turned his head and winked at her.

"Look at that," Sally breathed reverently as his next one landed on the other side of Regina's arrow.

Then he shot the third one.

Regina stared in shock as his arrow not only hit hers but sliced it in two.

"Got you," said the earl, showing his fine teeth in a wide grin. "What a shame. You might have done well if it weren't for me."

Might have, indeed. He was taunting her. "Enjoy yourself now," she snapped. "You'll never shoot arrows here again after I marry your uncle."

"Do you think so?" the earl said coolly. "I don't think so. When my uncle realizes that you're just an untutored child who has no use for him, he won't want to marry you. Then it will be some more suitable female who presides here, one who appreciates his sterling qualities rather than his gold, Miss Hammond, and who appreciates me. In other words, it definitely won't be you."

"It might be worth it if I never had to see you again, my lord," she said before lifting her bow and bringing it down

over his head. Regina gazed at her handiwork, and then she
began to giggle. "You look silly," she said.

Blazing blue eyes stared into her own. "You shouldn't
have done that, Miss Hammond." The earl paused after
each word. "Beware. The next contest will go to me."

Regina turned away so that he would not see the fright in
her eyes—or the hot lick of excitement.

~Chapter 3

EARLY THE NEXT morning the earl sat by himself on the stone terrace outside of his uncle's library. Dressed for riding in a dark blue frock coat, doeskin breeches, and Hessian boots, he looked as though he must be waiting for his horse to be brought up so that he could go for a gallop. No such thought was on his mind, however; he had taken himself off to the terrace in order to be alone, to sort out his thoughts. Those thoughts were about Miss Regina Hammond.

He should be ashamed of himself, he decided, being at daggers drawn with someone so much less worldly than he. Unfortunately, however, he was not ashamed, although there were some other descriptions that would fit his state: frustration at having been temporarily bested, anger for allowing a chit just out of the schoolroom to have the last word, and a feeling of being intrigued. Definitely Miss Hammond intrigued him.

Besides, she wasn't an innocent in her effect on men. No, like Lilith and other infamous temptresses he could name, she was innately alluring, tantalizing, and seductive—which was not to imply that he found her appealing, he told himself, because he did not.

He knitted his dark brows and scowled horribly.

"Why are you looking so fierce?" his uncle asked, coming out onto the terrace to join him. He flipped up the tails of his brown coat, then sat down in a wicker chair next to the one inhabited by his nephew. "Or are you just thinking in what part of his anatomy you would like to shoot that deer?"

"What deer?" the earl asked, thereby answering his uncle's question.

Mr. James smiled gently. "That is what I surmised. Won't you tell me what is troubling you?"

Naturally the earl had no intention of informing his uncle that he was thinking unkind thoughts about Miss Hammond. "It's nothing, really," he said as he stretched his long legs out before him and stared thoughtfully at the tassels on his boots. "I was just wondering how we were to entertain Miss James and Miss Hammond today. It is no easy thing trying to keep children constantly occupied."

It was Mr. James's turn to frown. "I wish you would stop calling Miss Hammond a child," he said. "After all, she is old enough to be introduced to society."

"That is true," the earl agreed, pulling in his legs and rising. "The problem is that as far as providing amusement to those two, we must think of them as children—restless, energetic children who might well get into mischief if left to their own devices."

Mr. James shuddered. "I forgot to tell you," he said. "I will not be able to accompany the three of you today. I have decided to devote myself to Mrs. Eckle and Mr. Hammond. After all, they are my guests, too."

"So they are," the earl agreed with a smile. "And perhaps you can rest a bit as well."

Mr. James did not appear to care for that suggestion. "I do not need to rest," he said, sounding peevish. "I am not ancient, you know. Indeed, I am but ten years older than you."

"Quite true, quite true," the earl murmured soothingly. "Would you care to join us later if we decide to walk back up that hill or to play tennis for a few hours?"

The very idea of doing such things seemed to horrify Mr. James. "No, I couldn't," he said in a faint voice. "Mrs. Hammond and Mr. Eckle, you know."

The earl did not correct his uncle's transposition of his guests' names. "Oh, yes, I forgot about them," he said.

"You will entertain my darling, though, won't you?"

The earl's fingers curled as though they longed to get

around a certain someone's throat. "I'll entertain her, all right. Don't worry about that."

"I won't," Mr. James said with his benign smile. "I know you have my best interests at heart, and Regina is my best interest. Do you not think so?"

He might if he thought it was in a man's best interest to enslave himself. Didn't his uncle realize that one should never fall in love with a woman who cared less for him than he cared for her? To do so was to be foolish beyond permission. Thank heaven, he'd never been involved in such a relationship; he was impervious to that sort of idiocy.

Thinking about enslavement made him think of Miss Eckle. "I have a problem," he told Mr. James abruptly, without bothering to answer his question—which he could not have answered anyway without offending his uncle mightily.

"Does it involve Miss Hammond?"

Steven laughed. "Truly, Uncle, most things in this world do not."

Mr. James tugged uncomfortably at his neckcloth as though it were cutting off his air. "I just thought . . ."

"No, it concerns Miss Hammond's little friend, Miss Eckle. I fear that she has developed a tendre for me."

"I have seen no evidence of that," Mr. James replied starchily. "If anything, she seems to favor me. You probably haven't noticed, but she's paid quite a bit of attention to me."

The earl spread his strong hands. "Nevertheless I have good reason to think my observation is correct."

"That's ridiculous," Mr. James replied, sounding excessively annoyed. "She's an unsophisticated girl, much, much too young for you." Presumably realizing that the same could be said about Regina in relation to him—only more so since he was older than the earl—Mr. James blushed and changed his tack. "I . . . uh . . . sometimes these things turn out all right," he said.

"I have no intention of having them turn out in any way at all," the earl told him severely.

"How do you know she cares for you?" Mr. James asked, sounding belligerent once more.

"I don't know it for a fact, but it seems apparent. She stares at me. She pats my hand if she thinks I'm distressed. She either rushes to talk to me or else shuts up like a clam when I'm in the vicinity. She blushes; she—"

"That's enough. I believe you. What are you going to do about it, Steven?"

The earl's expression was rueful. "I don't know. Do you have any suggestions?"

"I? No, I don't think so."

"Somehow I've got to redirect her feelings," the earl said.

"Are you certain that will succeed?" Mr. James asked dubiously. "Nothing could sway me from loving Miss Hammond; perhaps Miss Eckle loves you in the same way."

The earl's expression became grim. "Good Lord, I hope not."

Mr. James rubbed one of his soft hands against the other. "Poor little mite," he said sympathetically. "Unrequited love is the very devil."

The earl realized that his uncle Severn was talking not only about Miss Eckle but also himself. It was to be hoped that in another day or two he would have arrived at the conclusion that Regina Hammond was wrong for him.

Naturally those objections against his uncle marrying her did not apply to the earl himself, although it went without saying that she was not for him, either. His reasons, however, were different.

What are my reasons? he asked himself, frowning once more. Except for not wanting to be wed to anyone at all—a very good reason—he could not come up with a single one this time. The realization worried him.

With a scowl, he said, "I've got to make Miss Eckle see that she is wrong for me, or I am wrong for her. I'll think of some way to do it."

Cupping his hand to his chin, Mr. James sat and thought

about the problem. "Why not enlist someone else to help you?" he finally said.

"Someone else? Whom did you have in mind?"

"I don't know. Well, yes, I do—you need the help of a woman."

The earl hoped his uncle didn't mean Miss Hammond. "What woman?"

"A beautiful, sophisticated woman who will make Miss Eckle come to the awareness by herself that she is too young for you. You must know such a female."

"That is the *only* sort I know," the earl said with a cynical laugh.

"Good. Then collect one and bring her here. It should do the trick."

"I'll think about it." In his haste to go off again and do just that, the earl struck his hip against his chair. "Women," he said bitterly.

An hour later the earl had come up with a plan involving a beautiful, sophisticated woman named Lucy, the widow of old Lord Sanding. He had once had an enjoyable affair with her, which had terminated quite amicably. He felt certain she would be willing to take it up again, if not otherwise engaged.

Sitting down in a large tapestry-covered wing chair in his bedroom, he wrote a note to the lovely Lucy, who, if he were in luck, was still in residence at her country place not too far from his uncle's house. Then he called for a groom to deliver it. There was no time to waste. After that, he went off to collect the two young ladies.

Like him, they had dressed to go riding. He gave Miss Eckle's costume a cursory glance, so that although he could have explained, if asked, that she wore brown, he could not have drawn a picture of anything she had on. Miss Hammond was an altogether different tale. He was aware not only that her riding habit was red but also that it was trimmed down the front with silver braid. And he could have described the black beaver hat that sat on her beautiful hair down to the silver cord and silver tassels that decorated it. He was most aware, however, that the colors accentuated her pale skin and large, dark eyes.

Miss Eckle batted her skimpy eyelashes at the earl, who pretended not to notice. "Where is Mr. James, my lord?" she asked brightly into the silence. "He is going with us, isn't he?"

The earl shook his handsome head, at the same time wondering why she asked about their host first thing—and Miss Hammond did not. What this difference told about Miss Eckle he could not fathom, but it was clear to him what it told about Miss Hammond. She did not care tuppence for his uncle. He was doing the right thing by trying to free Mr. James from her tentacles. If he hadn't been altogether confident before that what he was doing was correct, he was now.

Coolly he said, "He is going to entertain your mother and Mr. Hammond today."

"Good heavens, I hope they don't gamble," said Regina with all the passion he thought she would have expressed concerning Mr. James's absence. "That is how I got into—" Abruptly she broke off her statement. "Perhaps I should stay with them."

"No," the earl said loudly, then repeated more quietly, "No." Though it might be like pouring oil on a fire for him to be alone with Miss Eckle, that was not his reason for protesting. The idea of not being with Miss Hammond bothered him. Probably, he thought, it was because she was still one up on him and he wanted to even the score. "Shall we ride now?" he asked.

Regina ignored him. Putting her hand into a sack she carried, she pulled out some seeds and crumbs, as she had the previous day. Then she whistled.

A curious jay flew to a close-by tree limb to observe her. Spying the crumbs, he alit on her wrist.

"Come on," Regina coaxed in a soft, loving voice such as she'd never used yet when addressing Lord Audlin or his uncle. "Come, little darling." She pursed her lips as though she wanted to kiss the vibrant bundle of bones and brown-pink feathers.

His Lordship stared in fascination as the bird cocked its head and looked at her with one beady eye. Then it hopped onto Regina's palm and began to eat.

A wave of something very like jealousy welled up in the Earl of Audlin again. Why did she talk so nicely to a bird? Look how one of her fingers went out and gently stroked the creature's chest over its fast-beating heart. She'd probably rather die than touch the sleeve of his coat.

"We haven't all day," he said reprovingly. "The horses are waiting."

Regina gave him a scathing look, but shook her hand lightly, scattering the rest of the crumbs and seeds and causing the jay to fly off.

None of them spoke as they mounted their horses, although Regina continued to glare at Steven. He felt heat burn along the back of his neck. Let her look at him like that, he thought angrily. Her opinion of him counted for nothing.

Forgetting that Sally needed to be dissuaded from loving him, he favored her with a friendly grin. His white teeth flashed.

"Oh," she said, putting a hand to her throat as though somehow her heart had gotten lodged in it. "Oh, my."

"Hurry, Sally," Regina said sharply. "Let us not dawdle."

They continued to ride, mostly in silence, for near to an hour. Then they turned back. By that time the sun had burned the lingering haze off of the fields and the chill from the air. "May we stop here?" Regina asked when they were but a short distance from the house. "I'd like to get down for a while."

The place she chose was a wide field, thick with grasses and the pinks, blues, and yellows of early wildflowers. It smelled sweet, the way she did. After accepting the earl's help in dismounting, she let go of his hand and spun around. "It's lovely here," she said, then closed her eyes and let herself be enfolded in the light, like an exotic flower in love with the sky.

He did not remember doing it, but he must have helped

Miss Eckle down, too, because she came to stand beside
Regina. Her red hair blazed in the sun's rays.

A rose and a radish, thought the earl, regarding the two
girls. But it was the rose, not the radish, he hungered to
taste.

What could have put that thought into his head? He must
be losing his mind. Disgusted with himself, he gave a
preoccupied sweep of his hand toward the grass in invitation
to the young women, then sat down and leaned back against
one of the few shade trees growing there.

When he glanced up, he saw Regina through a wash of
luminescence. Though it was merciless, it found no flaw in
her. She was beautiful in the sun.

He watched as she bent to pick some flowers. Her dark
curls fell forward to frame her face. Her expression was
absorbed, unaware. Suddenly he felt his loins tighten with
desire.

He almost groaned aloud. It was Bedlam next for
him—unless he availed himself of the services of a woman.
Obviously that was what he was in need of. Perhaps he
should consider resuming his affair with Lucy when she
arrived, he thought, his mind on himself and his sudden,
insane obsession with Miss Hammond. Never mind Miss
Eckle, or his uncle Severn, either; he needed Lucy for his
own sake.

"We should go back," he said abruptly as he got to his
feet. Although Miss Eckle agreed, Regina insisted stubbornly that she was not ready to leave. Lord Audlin
frowned. "We are going," he said.

It was several minutes before he realized that Miss
Hammond was not following him. The jade must have
stayed behind, in the meadow. "Go on," he directed a
reluctant Miss Eckle. "The horse knows the way. I shall
fetch your friend."

Regina watched Sally and the earl ride off. How long
would it take before Lord Audlin realized she had disobeyed
him? Would he be angry? Would he even care?

Probably not, she thought. He had no interest in her other

than to ensure that she did not become affianced to his uncle. As for her, she had no interest in him other than to beat him at his game. Wasn't that true?

Being an honest person, she had to admit that her explanation wasn't altogether true. Despite herself, she found herself drawn to him, and not just because of her stupid, old daydreams. No, and not just because he was handsome and exciting, either, although he was both.

There was kindness in him, and caring; even in the short time she'd known him, she'd come to see that. Indeed, wasn't it his affection and concern for his uncle that caused the earl to disapprove of her?

Regina's dark brows drew down, as did her mouth. She mustn't forget that he stood in opposition to her. She *wouldn't* like him, she told herself; she wouldn't.

A faint nearby movement made her turn her head. Seeing a rabbit stare at her from a clump of primroses, she pulled some grasses from the ground next to her and put them in her lap. "Come on," she cajoled in a gentle voice; "come on."

The little animal took a few tentative steps toward her, then ran back through the primroses and disappeared. Something had frightened him off.

Regina knew what it was. It was the same something that was frightening her, the sound of a horse. It was the earl's horse, with the earl sitting atop it, his face like a thundercloud.

"So there you are," he scolded. "Get on your horse this instant, Miss Hammond, and follow me." Regina made no effort to move. "Do you hear me, Miss Hammond? I am responsible for you and have no intention of leaving you here alone. It might not be safe."

"Where is Miss Eckle?" Regina said, rising.

Although her question seemed innocuous, it was obvious from her tone that it was no question at all. It was a way of saying that if it was safe for Sally Eckle to ride alone, it was equally safe for Regina to stay in the meadow. She was calling the earl a liar; and from the flush on his face, he knew it.

The earl bit his lip before saying in a deceptively calm voice, "She is probably with my uncle by now, although he is no more enamored of having to amuse children than I."

Why had she thought he was kind? "Indeed?" she said, flushing. "How fortunate it is, then, that the 'children' find you just as boring as you do them, my lord, if not more so."

"Is that so?" the earl said between clenched teeth.

Regina could see she had drawn blood. Her smile was as triumphant as though she were responsible for having held off several ravaging armies. "It is," she answered sweetly.

The earl abruptly got down from his horse. His lips tight, he drew close to Regina. Her dark eyes widened and she backed away.

"There is no place where you can go to escape," the earl said relentlessly.

"I . . . what do you mean?"

Lord Audlin's handsome face was unyielding. "You have been very rude to me, Miss Hammond. I am not used to people being rude to me. I am waiting for you to apologize."

Regina's stubborn little chin went out. "Never," she said.

"Then I fear you must be taught a lesson."

The chin elevated. "Don't you touch me."

"Not touch you? Oh, yes, I'm going to touch you, where and as much as I please."

Regina started to back away. "I'll tell my papa. I'll tell your uncle."

"Go right ahead, my *dear* Miss Hammond."

With that, he pulled her into his arms. She could feel the whole length of his body against her. His arms tightened. He bent his head and found her lips.

She made them rigid, ungiving, as prim as a Puritan's. The earl, it became obvious, was not daunted. His mouth pressed down hard on hers. Regina whimpered.

At once the earl's lips gentled, and instead of plundering, they began to coax her for what he wanted. Regina sighed and then, as if there were no other choice, her arms crept around his neck and her body softened against his.

After a while she felt her heart pound and heard the blood roar in her ears. She felt a longing, too—for something. Suppose he were to lower her to the ground, there in the meadow, in the hot sun and with the sweet smells of flowers and green, growing things? They could be close, so close. She wanted that.

She felt the earl stiffen and move away from her. "I hope that you will have learned something from that," he said, sounding more bewildered than pedagogical. "Come, Miss Hammond." Without looking directly at her, he lifted her onto her horse, after which he mounted his. "It is time to go," he said, turning his steed toward the house.

Without another word, he rode off. Regina licked her lips, full and red from his kisses. She felt dazed and bereft. She stared at Lord Audlin's broad back, before raising her delicate shoulders in a gesture of confusion. "I'm sorry, Sally," she murmured. "I . . . I forgot he was your love." Then, only because she did not know what else to do, she followed him.

They returned to the house without having spoken, her horse still trailing behind his. She intended to say something to him, to ease the almost palpable tension; it was the civilized thing to do. She might even have apologized for not agreeing to his original request to ride back with him and Sally. She did not have the chance, however, because Sally came outside just at that moment, smiled blindingly at the earl, and then went to her friend.

Regina tried one more time the next day, but gave it up when a carriage drew up to the house just as she was about to begin a well-rehearsed speech. From the excited expression on his face when he saw the carriage, Lord Audlin wouldn't have listened to her words anyway.

The cause of his indifference to Regina was a beautiful blond woman dressed in a black cloak, a black-and-white-striped carriage dress, and a white bonnet with a green ribbon that exactly matched her sloe eyes. She was surrounded by a battery of black trunks, white bandboxes, and black-and-white jewel cases. Lady Sanding, the earl's secret weapon, had arrived.

Lady Sanding stepped away from her shiny black coach with its two pair of white horses, and looked about her. "Steven," she said. "Oh, my dear, this is wonderful." Putting her slender gloved hand in his, she leaned over and kissed him. The two young ladies clutched each other's hands as they watched him return the woman's kiss with enthusiasm.

"Come up to our bedroom, Regina," Sally said in an agonized whisper as she tugged at Regina's dress. "Do, please."

"Very well," Regina replied, sounding equally agonized.

Once inside their room, Sally threw herself ungracefully onto the bed. "Did you see her?" she wailed. "Is she not the most beautiful creature you've ever looked at, besides you, that is?"

Regina opened and closed her mouth, apparently not knowing how to answer the question.

"She is, isn't she?" Sally said when Regina still did not reply. "Do you think she's his mistress?"

Regina's dark brows went up and she gasped. "Do you think so?"

"It's possible," said Sally. "You know how men are."

Regina believed she did now, after having been kissed by the earl. For a second or two she worried that he might have caused her to be increasing, but she forced the hideous thought from her mind. "He'd never bring his mistress here," she said, hoping that what she said was fact. "It is not done."

"That's true, isn't it?" Sally agreed with a sigh of relief. "Then who can she be? I know she can't be his sister. No man ever kissed his sister like that. Nor can she be the wife of a friend, for the same reason. Oh, Regina, what shall I do?"

"Forget him," Regina spat. "He is not worthy of touching your shoe."

"Oh, yes, he is—and my foot and my ankle, as well," Sally replied. "I wouldn't mind at all."

"I am not sure that I would, either," Regina said with evident self-loathing.

"Regina, what do you mean? Do you wish Mr. James would touch your shoe?"

Her friend stared at her as though she had no idea as to the identity of the aforementioned Mr. James. Then she flushed. "No. No," she repeated more loudly. "I do not mean anything. I don't know what I mean."

"Regina Hammond, you sound as addlepated as I. Do not tell me that you are in love, too."

"I won't," Regina said wearily.

Sally took a step toward the door, then stepped back. "You must come to the saloon with me to meet her," she said. "I simply cannot do it by myself."

"I don't want to. I'm not well. I have the headache. I . . ."

She did not finish. A message from Mrs. Eckle demanding the presence of the two girls was delivered by her maid. In a feverish whirl of activity, they changed into pretty muslin frocks, Sally's with a ruff about the neck and Regina's filled in with a habit shirt. They pinched their cheeks and had their hair brushed. After that, they obediently, if reluctantly, went down the stairs to be introduced.

After making their curtsies, they sat together on a gold, Greek-style settee that was off to one side and looked glumly at Lady Sanding, who after smiling in an offhand way at them, went back to talking to the three gentlemen.

"She must be as old as the earl," Sally whispered. "You'd think he would have better taste."

Regina grimaced. "You'd think my papa would."

Both of them studied Mr. Hammond's expression, which was as pleased looking as that of the other two men. "I'm surprised at him," Regina added.

Mrs. Eckle leaned forward from her chair and glared at the young women. Immediately they turned away from each other.

Just then Lady Sanding raised her head and gave the other females a conspiratorial wink and a smile that seemed to say, Aren't men silly?

"She's nice," Sally muttered, as though that were the crowning indignity.

Regina's mouth turned down. "I agree."

Lady Sanding beckoned to them with a leisurely wave of her hand. "Do come closer and join us," she said. "It won't be any fun without you."

"What won't, Lucy?" the earl asked in a tone that said clearly that he found her amusing and charming.

"Anything."

The men laughed appreciatively. Even Mr. James seemed to have forgotten that he'd given his heart away to Regina.

"Trolls!" Regina muttered. How she longed to leave this room. Every other person in it, in one way or another, distressed her. Even her dear friend Sally distressed her. Whenever she looked at Sally, she felt guilty for having allowed the earl to kiss her. And even if she hadn't exactly allowed him, she'd enjoyed his kisses prodigiously. If only Mrs. Eckle would permit her to go; but Regina knew she would not.

"Have you girls had your come-outs yet?" Lady Sanding asked.

"No, my lady," they replied in unison.

Her Ladyship smiled. "How quaint. I remember when I had my come-out. I had a glorious time."

"Of course you did," the earl said, putting his hand on her arm. "You were the Incomparable that year—and still are."

Regina hadn't realized how much she disliked Lady Sanding, nice or not. She had a strong desire to slap the earl's hand off of her arm and burst into tears.

"Hussy," Sally murmured out of the side of her mouth.

Regina choked, then began to laugh. She did not want to, but she could not help herself.

It was amazing what an effect her mirth had on the various members of their group. Sally giggled, her mama frowned awfully, and the men looked puzzled. As for Lady Sanding, she laughed, too, showing perfect, white teeth. Regina could have throttled her.

"There is nothing like a good laugh," Lady Sanding announced. "Steven, do you remember the time we went to Vauxhall, you and I, and each of us chose the fattest person there to dance with? Yours was a seamstress, or so she said, and mine was a banker.''

"Or so he said," Steven replied, then fell to laughing with her. The other two men joined in.

"They make me sick," Sally said, once again out of the corner of her mouth.

It was the earl's turn to reminisce. "Do you remember the night we went to a masquerade ball and you were dressed as an organ grinder?"

"Yes, and I had borrowed a monkey from a real organ grinder."

"Yes, you had," he said appreciatively. "And it tried to eat the fruit on Lady Badley's headdress. What was she supposed to be, anyway?"

Lady Sanding put her hand to her exquisite face. "The goddess of nature, I believe. However, when she discovered the monkey, she sounded more like a fishwife."

Again, the three gentlemen laughed.

"Brazen thing!" Sally whispered to her friend. "Regina, I don't believe I can bear much more of this."

Neither could Regina. "Stand up, Sally," she said, giving her friend's thigh a push. "We are ever so sorry," she said more loudly, making sure not to look at Mrs. Eckle. "We must beg to be excused now. We need to . . . need to finish writing our letters."

Mrs. Eckle's pale eyebrows rose almost to her hairline. She started to say something, but then bit her lip.

The earl was not so reticent. "To whom?" he demanded.

It was an odd thing for him to say, but it was forgotten when Regina's papa added, "Yes, to whom?"

Regina gave him a sparkling smile. "Oh, Papa, you've forgotten already. Come, Sally." Grabbing her friend's hand, she half dragged her from the room.

It was as well she did that. Not a minute after they returned to the privacy of their bedroom, Sally began to cry. Regina poked around until she found a handkerchief and then handed it to her friend.

"Thank you," Sally said into the handkerchief before

blowing her nose. "Oh, Regina, what am I going to do? He'll never want me now."

Although a certain amount of information was left out of this *cri de coeur,* Regina understood exactly what her friend meant. She shook her head. "I don't know," she said. "I agree that you are faced with a difficulty."

"Difficulty? It's an impossibility."

Regina quite concurred, would have concurred even before Lady Sanding had arrived, but she could hardly say so to Sally. "You could be wrong," she said doubtfully. "Surely he will come to appreciate your finer qualities."

"Compared to her, I don't have any," Sally wailed. "Did you notice her bosom?"

"Bosoms aren't everything," Regina said bracingly.

Sally gave her a doleful look. "They are if you don't have one. My mama said I would, but I am still waiting. The question is, will the earl wait? I fear I know the answer."

Regina shook her head with exasperation. "The answer is that you should not love the earl. He is not worthy of you."

"Of course he is," her red-haired friend said indignantly. "He is so handsome. Have you looked at his eyes? They give me the fever."

Regina had looked *into* his eyes, and she, too, had been overcome by fever. Let she who is without fever cast the first stone, she thought in guilty confusion, and clamped her lips closed.

~Chapter 4

THE NEXT DAY Regina rose early and took her cup of hot chocolate to the small morning room she'd previously discovered on a tour of Fairways. She liked it because it faced south and gave a pretty view of the park from its light-filled windows.

She sat facing the view, her hands folded in the lap of her white-and-blue sprigged-muslin dress. Her feet, in blue slippers, were set neatly together on the floor. Except for the fact that she was quite beautiful, she looked just like any other well-brought-up young lady with nothing to occupy her.

In truth, however, she was occupied. She was thinking about the import of Lord Audlin kissing Lady Sanding's hand—twice!—when the two of them had been standing outside the dining-room door earlier. She knew that they were old friends, of course, but was it necessary to kiss an old friend's hand, and not once but twice? Surely such behavior was excessive.

She held up her own hand and looked at it. She had to admit that it would not have distressed her if the earl had kissed it even four or five times. A kiss on the neck would not have been amiss, either. Or one . . .

What was the matter with her? Had she been eating too many stimulating foods? The meals were more heavily spiced at Fairways than she was used to.

Shamefaced, she stared down at the Turkey carpet that covered a portion of the floor. It was absurd for her to try to blame the food. She knew perfectly well it wasn't the menu that was causing her blood to heat; it was the earl. She was definitely drawn to him—but she had better stay away from him.

A noise, the creaking of one of the wide floorboards perhaps, caused her to glance toward the door. Her pleasant haven was being invaded.

"Oh, no," she said, looking up at the earl, "it's you."

"So it is," he agreed with a bow, his perfectly fitting blue Bath coat stretching across his broad back as he did. His tight gray breeches showed off his lean hips and long thighs. His boots shone. He was a handsome sight, devastatingly male and slap up to the echo.

For a moment admiration gleamed in her dark eyes. No hint of praise appeared in her voice when she spoke, however. "I do not mean to be rude," she said, "but I do not wish company."

"That is too bad, and you are being rude," the earl replied, his grin taking some of the sting out of his words. "I am here and intend to stay."

Regina got up from her seat. "In that case, I shall leave, my lord."

As quick as a cat, Lord Audlin crossed the intervening space and took hold of her arm. "No, don't leave. In truth, I was looking for you. There is something I need to ask you."

Regina did not want him to touch her. It was not just his kisses that disturbed her. "Take your hand from my arm, or I'll scream down the house," she said.

A look of disapproval flickered on the earl's visage. "You are always threatening me, Miss Hammond. It is an unbecoming trait."

"When did I threaten you before?" she blustered.

"Do you really want me to tell you?"

It was apparent from her expression and the crimson color that flooded her face that Regina remembered. She had told him that if he kissed her, she would inform his uncle and her papa. He'd kissed her anyway—but she hadn't said a word to them.

"You are right," she said, lowering her eyes. "I have threatened you, but it is your fault. If you weren't such a pirate, I would not need to."

"A pirate?" The earl rocked back on his heels and laughed. "You are a surprising girl," he said when he stopped. "Why do you dislike me so much?"

"I don't dislike you."

"Really?"

She shook her head, wanting to smile. She would not, however. The earl was far too sure of himself. He needed a set-down for his own good. "If anything, I would say that I am indifferent to you."

Instead of responding with anger, Lord Audlin grinned again. "I am not so certain of that, Miss Hammond," he told her in a low, husky voice. "When I kissed you yesterday . . ."

"That meant nothing," she said, praying that she would not blush, "at least no more than the kisses you placed on Lady Sanding's hand."

Lord Audlin's heavy brows lowered over his eyes. "What are you talking about, Miss Hammond?"

She had said too much. "Nothing. I was ragging you, but I shouldn't have been. I am very sorry."

He ignored her words as though she hadn't spoken them. "You were spying on me, me and Lady Sanding, weren't you?"

"I did not do any such thing," she said indignantly. "Why would I? I have no interest at all in what you do, with her or anyone else. I merely happened to be glancing down the hall, and I saw you."

Lord Audlin put a thumb under her chin and pushed it up so that she had to look into his eyes. "At least it wasn't that silly little friend of yours. I've caught her peering out at me a number of times. It gives me an eerie feeling."

"If you mean Sally," she responded coldly, knocking his thumb away, "she is not silly; and I do not appreciate your referring to her as such. Furthermore she does not peer."

For the first time since she'd met him, he gave her a look of complete approval. "You're a loyal one, aren't you?"

She nodded. "Of course."

"Good. So many females aren't."

Suddenly Regina felt shy; she was unused to the earl viewing her with favor. Her eyes lowered again, but she allowed her mouth to soften at the corners.

Lord Audlin leaned his hip against a walnut table and crossed his arms. His blue eyes studied her. "As I said before, you are full of surprises, Miss Hammond."

"Am I? Why do you think so?"

It was the earl's turn to seem, not shy precisely, but restrained. "I don't know. You are such a mix of child and woman, diffidence and pluck, you confuse me. I never know whether I should hand you a dolly or—" His voice broke off, but the words *make love to you,* though not spoken, hung in the air.

"I'll take the dolly," she said quickly, in an effort to alter the now charged atmosphere.

The earl stretched out his hands and said with a smile, "I shall get you one. Is there a possibility that we can be friends, Miss Hammond?"

She held back before allowing her hands to disappear within his. "Perhaps we can."

He rubbed a thumb softly against one of her palms. "Let us both try." When she nodded, he said, "Good. Then perhaps you will not mind answering a few questions. They might make you angry—but I hope they will not."

Regina stiffened ever so slightly. "Yes?"

Lord Audlin's pleasant, approving expression did not change, nor did he stop stroking her palm. "Has my uncle asked you to marry him yet?" She shook her head no. "Do you mean to accept him if he does?"

"Is there some reason why I should not, my lord?" she said softly.

The earl hesitated. "Because I truly believe you are wrong for each other."

"Indeed? Is there someone you know who is right for him?"

He shook his head in the negative.

"Is there someone you know, then, who is right for me?"

Lord Audlin shifted his weight so that his face was close to hers. His blue eyes took on a heavy-lidded, lazy look. Just as quickly, however, he backed off. "No, there is not. I don't doubt, though, that you will find that person eventually. Maybe even soon."

"Really?"

"Why, yes." He retreated a few more paces, like someone who senses he is in danger. "How about that fellow who stands outside your London town house every day?"

It was as though he had struck her. "He would be willing," she said, her voice like ice, "just as Lady Sanding would probably be willing to have you."

The earl lowered his dark brows. "Why do you keep mentioning Lady Sanding to me? What does she have to do with anything?"

"Only you would know that," Regina said sharply.

Lord Audlin reddened. "You may appear to some to be an angel, Miss Hammond, but you are not. You are a baby viper. Take my word for it."

"Why am I more of one than you, my lord? You think you can say anything to me and it will be acceptable, but I am not to say peep to you."

"If it were peep," he said angrily, "I would not mind. But, no, you must always have the last word—and a harsh word it is."

They stood and traded fulminating looks, blue eyes and brown shooting daggers, until the sound of someone entering the room made them move apart. It was Lady Sanding, looking lovely in a black-and-white-striped gown with a frilled white apron atop it. "How nice," she said in a cheerful voice. "It always gives me pleasure to see friends enjoying themselves together."

Both Regina and the earl looked at her as though she were mad. Then Lord Audlin laughed mirthlessly. "You are mistaken, Lucy. We are not friends, nor are we enjoying ourselves." Over his shoulder, Lady Sanding winked at

Regina, as though to say that the earl should not be taken seriously.

"I have been waiting here for you," he said. Bending, he took up Regina's chocolate and drained the cup. Then he put Lady Sanding's hand on his arm and escorted her from the room, not looking behind him even once.

"You, you," Regina sputtered. She stared at her empty cup with fury—knowing full well, however, that it was not the chocolate about which she was angry. Waiting for Lady Sanding, was he? Was that the truth? He had told Regina earlier he had been looking for her. Had she been but a diversion to while away the time until Lady Sanding appeared?

Oddly she found that she was more furious with the black-and-white-clad Lady Sanding, who had been quite nice, than with the earl. "Zebra," she muttered. She picked up a book from a nearby table and threw it against the wall.

"Oh, my," said a voice she recognized as belonging to Mr. James. He picked up the book, dusted it off, and returned it carefully to the table. "Perhaps I should come back later, my dear."

Regina glared at him. She did not wish to have more company; she was still recovering from the earl's visit—and Lady Sanding's.

It was not surprising that Mr. James looked ready to jump into the hall. "I'm sorry," he said.

Her look changed to one of surprise. "For what?"

"I don't know, but it is apparent that something has upset you. I must always be sorry for that."

What a dear man he was. But how she wished her papa had never met him. That was not just because Mr. James seemed more like a kindly uncle than a beau, either. More important was that if she hadn't met Mr. James, she wouldn't have met the disturbing Lord Audlin, and she could have held on to her daydreams, not to mention her poise and confidence.

Still, it wasn't Mr. James's fault that he had such a relative. "Thank you," she said gently. "Do you wish to see me about something, or have you come here to enjoy the warmth and sunshine of the room?''

Nervously he tapped one booted foot on the floor. ''Oh, no, not necessarily. That is . . . I mean I could talk to you some other time if this is not convenient for you.''

It was Regina's turn to feel apprehensive. She hoped he did not intend to declare himself. To say the truth, she had been quite relieved that since they had been at Fairways he had not alluded even once to his hope of wedding her.

Nor did he now, at least not overtly. ''Do you want to tell me what upset you?'' he asked. ''I am a good listener.'' When she did not answer, he said, all in a rush, ''I wish I had the right to protect you. I would see to it that nothing ever upset you.''

Regina's laugh sounded artificial even to her own ears. ''That is very kind. However, I do not believe it is possible—or even desirable. Being wrapped in cotton wool sounds suffocating, somehow.''

Mr. James looked distressed. ''No, oh, no, I would not want to suffocate you. I would want you to be as free as a butterfly—in a sense.''

''In a sense?'' This time her laugh was genuine. ''What does that mean?''

''May I?'' He came over to where she was sitting and pulled up a matching floral wing chair. ''Butterflies are beautiful but delicate creatures,'' he said. ''Their colors and designs are splendid, but their wings tear so easily. I would want you to be free, but I would want to ensure that your wings would not get torn. I would wish to protect you from such harm.''

Regina wanted both to laugh and to cry. She found Mr. James's analogy of herself as a butterfly absurd. He really had no idea of her true nature—unlike his nephew, who seemed to provoke her forthright tongue at every turn. The truth was, she had never been a butterfly. Because of her papa's fondness for gambling and her mama's unfortunate early death, she had had to become self-sufficient while she was still a caterpillar, as it were.

"Miss Hammond," Mr. James said, interrupting her musings. "Miss Hammond—Regina, if I may—have you thought at all about my proposal?"

Her luck had run out. "What proposal is that?" she asked in a low voice, hoping to put him off, if only for a few more minutes.

"The proposal I made to your papa the night I met you, that is, that I would like to take care of you and him."

Regina choked. "And . . . and him?"

"Well, yes. That is, no, not really, unless he needed help. I do not wish to cause you pain, but you know that sometimes he . . . um, needs help of a financial sort. I could assist him, and would willingly do so."

Mr. James was all too ready to help, first herself and then her papa. He was in love with the needy, she thought, but then she rejected the idea. She was no fool. She knew perfectly well that he was in love with her face and would not have had any interest in assisting her papa if he had not been the sire of the person to whom the face belonged.

"I don't think that is necessary," she said.

Instead of seeming reassured, Mr. James looked glum. "Oh, that is too bad. But . . . but, still, I need not be precluded from marrying you. Isn't that so?"

He'd said the terrible words. Now what was she to do?

After a few seconds of awkward silence, she said, "You are most kind, and I appreciate the honor you do me. However . . ."

"You needn't say it. I can guess the rest of what you mean. I shan't give up, though. I am convinced that it is merely too soon. I must not rush you. I am at fault. Will you forgive me?"

"I—"

"A man needs hope, Miss Hammond."

Regina sighed. "Very well. Hope if you must, sir."

With a dignified smile, Mr. James stood, bowed slightly, and backed out of the room.

"If one more person comes in here," Regina muttered to herself, "I will exit by the window. Oh, no."

"Regina?" her friend Sally said in a low, sad voice. "I have been looking everywhere for you. What are you doing here?"

Regina laughed. "I came here to be alone."

"I do not find that humorous. I need you." Sally pressed her hand against her throat, as though to force her heart down.

Regina stared at her. "Has something happened? Why do you need me?"

"I need you because of Lord Audlin, of course," Sally said with a touch of impatience. "I assumed you'd know that, since you are aware that he is the one I love."

"I beg your pardon. I should have," Regina replied with only a hint of a smile. "What has he done now to shatter your peace?"

"I was coming down the hall when I heard his voice. I jumped into the library and opened the door a crack so that I could see him and hear better."

"You peered at him!" Regina exclaimed, remembering the earl's accusation against her friend.

Sally gave her a queer look. "It's nothing to get excited about, Regina. If I did not 'peer,' as you call it, I would not know what he is doing. In any case, what he was doing was talking to Lady Sanding."

"Yes? What is wrong with that?"

"After he talked to her, she touched his lips with her fingers."

"She didn't!" Regina, too, now had her hand pressed against her throat.

Sally went over and hugged Regina. "That is one of the things I love about you," she said. "You enter into my feelings completely. If I didn't know differently, I would think you cared for the earl as much as I."

Regina flushed and averted her eyes.

"Oh, Regina," Sally wailed, returning to her previous lament, "what am I to do? There must be some way I can convince him that I am desirable and wonderful and that he should love me and not Lady Sanding."

Regina shook her head. "You are all those things, but he is too stupid to realize it, preferring, instead, a woman who, unlike you, is a flirt and a hussy. You must give him up, Sally."

"How can I do that?" Sally asked, wrinkling her unmarked forehead. "I do not have him."

"Yes, that's right." Regina smiled gently at her friend. "That will make it so much easier, don't you think?"

Sally looked at her with something approaching contempt. "You don't understand, Regina. I cannot give him up, as long as there is hope."

Sally sounded like Mr. James. Regina grimaced. "Even if he has invited Lady Sanding here to be his lover?"

Sally looked defeated, but then rallied and said firmly, "Certainly. He might grow tired of her, you know. She's old for a woman."

Regina sighed and clasped her hands in front of her. "I thought you had more pride than that."

"There you go again, not understanding. Love doesn't have pride. Love says 'I have to have' and 'I don't care.'"

"You're right," Regina said. "I must never have loved anyone, at least not in a romantic way." And never want to, she added under her breath.

For a moment Sally looked triumphant. Then her face fell. "I still do not know what to do. You've had experience with Mr. James. How did you get him to love you?"

Regina hesitated before saying, "I don't know—that is, I didn't do anything."

"I forgot," Sally said. "You don't have to, because you're beautiful."

"If that were true, the earl would love me as well. Every man would."

Sally shook her head. "The earl is a different case, because he already loves Lady Sanding, who is beautiful also."

For some reason Regina felt quite disturbed over her friend's pronouncement. "You have no proof he loves her," she said peevishly.

"You're forgetting that he let her touch his lips."

Yes, and he had kissed her hand twice that morning. Of course, he had also kissed Regina, and not on her hand, either. Her mouth tightened. "That could be . . . uh . . . desire," she said. "That is a feeling men experience. In truth, from a few things I've overheard, they can feel it even when they do not love a female. It is something peculiar to them."

"Really?" said Sally. "Thank you. You have helped me."

Regina looked at her blankly. "I have? How did I do that?"

"By enlightening me. I see my way clearly now. I shall make the earl desire me. That will be better than nothing, and if I am lucky, it will be the first step to victory."

Regina clutched at her friend's arm. "I . . . I don't think you should do that, if you even could. It might be dangerous."

Sally disregarded her remarks. "I shall stuff my zona with cloth. I cannot wait any longer for my bosom to grow."

Regina was definitely worried by now. She hated to see Sally disappointed, yet was unable to hope that her friend would succeed. Besides, what would she do with the earl if she did arouse his desire? She was sure that Sally had not thought that far. "Don't do it," she said.

"But, Regina, I have no choice. I need to try to make an effort to fix his interest. I must leave now."

"Where are you going?" Regina asked in alarm.

"I am going to look for Mr. James. He will understand my feelings."

Very likely he would, Regina thought.

She watched her friend open wide the door, and then stop. "Mr. James," Regina heard Sally say. "You are the very one I wanted to find." With a sob, she threw herself into his arms.

Regina could just glimpse Mr. James's face. It was white.

"My dear Miss Eckle, I am glad to see you, too. What can I do for you?"

Sally's voice was low. Regina bent forward. "You must let me talk to you. I need to talk to someone sensible like you."

"There, there," Regina heard Mr. James's soothing voice say. "You must tell me all about it."

Regina cringed. She could not bear to stay in the room any longer. Who knew who would come in to importune her next? She had to get outside and away from people. She went into the hall, which, fortunately, was empty, then through the green baize door, and down into the kitchen.

"Lawks," the cook said, dropping a long-handled fork onto the grate. "You took me by surprise."

Regina pulled a sack out of a pocket while smiling at the woman. "I'm sorry. I was wondering if I might have some crumbs of your delicious bread to add to my seeds for the birds."

"You certainly do like to feed birds, miss. You should have a bird of your own, a linnet, maybe. They sing real good."

"I had one, but I could not bear to keep it caged up. It seemed so sad. I had to let it go," Regina said apologetically.

"You're a softhearted one. Well, here's your crumbs. Have a nice time. And, miss, don't go too far from the house. A girl like you shouldn't be out alone, not even here."

Regina sighed. There was more than one type of cage, she thought. Being a female was confining. Being a female with a pretty face was even worse, at least as far as freedom went. No wonder she didn't like to keep a bird in a cage.

Taking her sack, now plump with food, she went a little way into the park and stopped, remembering the cook's admonition. Besides, being just where she was, was lovely. It smelled clean and fresh, and she enjoyed the way the light filtered through the treetops. Visibly more relaxed, she filled her hand from the sack and then whistled. In only a little time, a sandy-brown skylark came to her and perched upon her finger.

"Hello," she said in the dulcet voice she seemed to reserve for nonhuman creatures. "Are you hungry, darling? I have something good here for you."

The bird jumped onto her palm and began to nibble. Regina smiled. It gave her such pleasure to be among nature's inhabitants and away from people, especially male people, who only seemed to want to cause her trouble.

She touched the bird's breast gently with a finger. Its covering of feathers was soft and warm. She could feel its heart beating. She smiled.

A moment later the bird cocked its head and then flew away. "I am sorry about that," Lord Audlin said from somewhere nearby. "He must have seen me and been frightened off."

Regina whirled around. "It doesn't matter," she said breathlessly. "Excuse me. I must go."

The earl closed the distance between them and put a restraining hand on her arm. "You cannot mean that I am scaring you off as well."

"You do not scare me at all." Her tone was scornful. "It is just that I do not wish to be insulted again so soon."

His smile was rueful. "I am sorry. I do not know why you have that effect upon me. In truth, with everyone else I am as docile as a lamb."

Regina giggled.

"I am. Will you forgive me?"

Instead of replying to that question, Regina said, "Where is Lady Sanding?"

The earl looked irritated. "I don't know. I am not the lady's keeper, Miss Hammond."

"Are you not? It doesn't matter. I will forgive you, my lord. Nevertheless I would like to be alone for a while. I've had ever so many people talk to me today, and it is still just morning."

"I don't wish to talk to you," he said cheerfully, bringing

a look of pique to Regina's face. "What I want to do is to get a bird to perch on my hand."

"You?" she asked in disbelief.

"Certainly I. Why not?"

Regina shrugged her slender shoulders. "You do not seem the sort to me who would enjoy it. Besides, I do not believe you can do it. Hardly anyone can, you know."

He kicked at a pebble lying on a leaf. "I believe that if you can, I can."

"Is that so?" she hooted. "I beg to dispute that."

"Would you care to make a wager, Miss Hammond?"

Regina's brows rose. "Why should I?"

"A little risk adds spice to life."

"Very well," she said, her eyes mischievous. "If you can entice a bird to eat from your hand, I will—"

"Just a minute," he said with a laugh. "I did not say that I would try to entice a bird to eat from my hand, but only to perch on my hand."

"Very well. If you can entice a bird to perch on your hand, I will . . ."

He looked at her intently. "What?"

"I do not know. I have nothing with which to wager."

"You are too modest, Miss Hammond."

Regina blushed, but then said, "Very well, if you can get a bird to perch on your hand, I will make you a fine handkerchief."

If he had any sense, the earl thought, he would accept the handkerchief as his reward. But he did not seem to have any sense. What he wanted was a kiss from those full, deeply red lips. "Thank you, but I do not need another handkerchief." His eyes looked laughingly into hers. "If I succeed, you must give me a kiss."

Regina was having a great deal of fun jousting verbally with Lord Audlin. This was so much better than being at odds with him. There was more, too, a feeling of delicious danger that was otherwise absent from her life. Unfortunately there was also that same loyalty the earl and she had talked about earlier. Sally would feel betrayed if Regina let the earl kiss her, even in a spirit of fun. "No," she said. "If I lose, I promise to sing for you and the others tonight."

"Come, Miss Hammond, what sort of forfeit is that? The kiss is better."

"You know you cannot win," she said.

"Then you have nothing about which to worry. Take a chance, Miss Hammond. It will do you good."

"Very well," she said with a blush, "but what will your forfeit be if you do not succeed?"

"If I do not succeed, I will give you a kiss."

Regina started to laugh. "If you win, I lose, and if you lose, I lose. You are a devil, my lord. In any case, I do not accept your forfeit."

"Very well. Then what shall it be?"

She tapped a finger against her mouth as if deep in thought. "I know. If you lose, you must read to us tonight. I'm certain you must own one book whose words would be acceptable to a female's ears."

"My uncle does. Very well. I agree to the challenge. May I?" he asked, pointing to the sack of seeds and bread that lay now on the ground. "This is what I will use to lure the bird."

"Certainly."

The earl poured some of the contents of the pouch into his hand. Then he whistled. Nothing happened.

Regina threw back her head and laughed. "I fear you lose, my lord."

"No, no," he protested. "I'm just beginning. You must give me time."

Again, he whistled. When there was no avian response, he said, "This is not a good spot."

"It was good enough for me a few minutes ago. I believe that no matter what you say, you do not have a chance, my lord."

"I will not concede. What it is, I think, is that you have already used up all the birds in this spot that perch on hands. Let us move farther down."

Regina accompanied him several yards to the right. Once more the earl stretched out his hand and whistled. With the other hand, he jerked at a string that was hanging down from the tree under which they stood. An instant later, a stuffed pheasant fell out of the tree. The earl caught it.

"Look at that," he said, clamping the pheasant's legs between his fingers and forcing it to stand upright. "I've won my wager." He threw the pheasant down. "It is time for you to pay up, Miss Hammond."

Regina was laughing so hard that she could not talk. The earl joined in. It took several minutes before they were able to speak without giving in to their mirth.

"You tricked me," she said. "You planned this whole thing, and you tricked me."

"I do not know why you say that."

He looked so comically affronted that Regina wanted to laugh again. She bit her lip. "I was right to call you a devil," she said. "I cannot believe that you went to so much trouble to fool me."

"Trouble?" he said, smiling. "This is nothing. If I were to tell you some of the elaborate tricks my friends have played on each other, you would consider yourself lucky that I only used a stuffed pheasant, Miss Hammond."

"Did you get it from your uncle?"

"Let us say that I got it from my uncle's smoking room, where it had been sitting for ages with nothing to do."

"But how did you know that I would be outside, feeding birds?"

He smiled. "When you were not in the house, I made that assumption."

Regina wanted to ask how he knew she was not in the house. Had he gone looking for her? After consideration, she decided that she did not want to ask after all. "I still cannot believe that you went to so much trouble," she said.

The earl's eyes fixed on her. "Never mind about that. It is time for me to claim your forfeit, Miss Hammond."

"I really don't think—"

"Good. Don't think. I won't either. Close your eyes."

Regina did as she had been bid, whereupon the earl's mouth came down to hers. She could feel his warm breath on her lips. "Kiss me," he murmured.

"I can't," said Regina, suddenly filled with anxiety. "Besides, you've already had enough affection today." She jerked away from him and fled.

"Miss Hammond?" he called after her, hoping she would change her mind and come back. While waiting, he absently put some of the seeds he still held into his mouth. Then he swallowed them, shells and all.

~Chapter 5

THE NEXT MORNING, Sally Eckle went looking for Mr. James. She wanted to discuss the earl with him. Regina had always been her confidante before; but though Sally still loved and valued her, she felt more comfortable with Mr. James.

She found her quarry in one of the ivy-covered walled gardens. He seemed to be deep in thought.

She walked over to him without his noticing her, so she tugged at the sleeve of his fine brown coat to gain his attention. "It's you," he said, a smile lighting up his face. "I was just wishing for some company. Will you go along with me for a stroll?" At once Sally fell into step with him.

"I wanted to thank you for your kindness to me yesterday," she said as she looked guilelessly into his eyes. "I don't know what I'd have done without our little talk. You kept up my spirits and gave me strength."

Mr. James appeared pleased by her words. "Thank you, my dear. It is good to know that I can be of some assistance to you." A doubting expressing crossed his face. "*Am* I of assistance? I do not see how I could be."

Absently Sally struck at a bee that was buzzing about her red hair. "Of course you are," she said. "I cannot talk to my mama; she would be horrified that I entertain deep feelings for a man, especially one who does not return them. I cannot talk to the earl. What would I say: 'I love you, my lord. Could you help me with this problem of mine?'"

She sighed heavily. "I cannot talk to Regina, either. She doesn't understand what is in my heart."

"That is probably because she has never been in love,"
Mr. James commented gloomily.

"I don't think that is it. I don't know why, but she seems
unable to find any good in the earl. In truth, I would say that
she dislikes him excessively."

Mr. James's forehead wrinkled in puzzlement. "How
odd. Most women adore him. Indeed, I can say without
exaggeration that females are always throwing themselves
at him. I could tell you stories. . . ." His voice petered out.
"I'm sorry. I forgot to whom I was speaking."

Sally turned out her hands in a gesture of hopelessness.
"It doesn't matter. Even if you hadn't told me, I would have
known it. How could women *not* do that? He is so very
handsome, so uncaring, so indifferent! And when one looks
into his eyes, one can detect the possibility that he could be
just a bit ruthless if he wished. What female could resist
such a wonderful, exciting man?"

To say that Mr. James gave the appearance of being
confused was an understatement. He ran his fingers haphaz-
ardly through his blond hair and blinked his eyes several
times. "Undoubtedly I have missed some sort of connection
among your thoughts, Miss Eckle. Naturally I can understand the handsome part. Why, however, would a woman
prefer an indifferent, uncaring man, with a possible capacity
for a bit of ruthlessness, to a feeling, caring one? I cannot
comprehend that."

Sally played with the double bow that decorated the front
of her peach muslin dress. "Perhaps it is because . . . or
maybe it is that . . . I cannot say, but so it is."

"Then there is no hope for me," Mr. James said sadly. "I
cannot act in those ways."

"Nor should you," she said. "You are different. You are
good. You are just the sort of papa every girl dreams of
having. I should know; I spend a lot of time dreaming about
a papa, because mine died when I was very young."

For some reason Sally could not fathom, Mr. James had
all the earmarks of someone who'd been terribly insulted.

"Did I say something wrong?" she asked.

He stared at and through her.

"Dear Mr. James, please don't look at me like that. I would never want to hurt you. I like you very much. You are my friend."

Mr. James rubbed his forehead, then forced his tautly held mouth to relax. "I know that when you say something, it is with all sincerity, and without malice. It is just my stupid vanity. Never mind."

If he hoped his words would make her feel better, he was doomed to disappointment: Sally began to cry. Tears trickled down over her freckles and landed on the cambric tucker with which she'd filled in the low neck of her gown.

Mr. James groaned. "Now what have I done?"

"You?" she said, groping for a handkerchief she could not find. "You haven't done anything. It is I."

"No, no, I've upset you." He handed her his handkerchief, then put an arm about her small shoulders and gave her a squeeze. "I would never want to do that. You are a very sweet girl. What is more, I do not know what I would do without these little talks either. You have become important to my sense of well-being."

The tears disappeared as rapidly as they had appeared. Sally beamed up at him. "That makes me happy to hear, especially since I don't mean a thing to the earl."

"We must stand together and remain friends," he said. "Is there any way that I can help you?"

Sally's laugh was mirthless. "You could tell me how to bring myself to the notice of Lord Audlin, who seems unaware of my existence. You could also tell me how to outshine Lady Sanding." She hesitated, then said, "I have an idea or two of my own—which I'm afraid I cannot share with you—but am in need of several more in case those do not work. What must I do?"

To her surprise, Mr. James seemed dreadfully embarrassed. He hemmed and hawed until finally he said, "I would not concern myself overmuch about Lady Sanding."

"She is beautiful," Sally protested, "and the earl adores her."

Once more he hesitated, before saying, "I know it seems

that way, but . . . but it might not be so. They are old, old
friends, and knew each other long ago.''

Sally said morosely, ''I suppose you mean that in the
biblical sense.''

''Miss Eckle!'' Mr. James's voice was shocked. ''I do
not know what to say to you!''

Sally seemed as though she were about to cry again.
''I've earned your disapproval, haven't I? I cannot bear it.''

''There, there,'' he said in a disarming voice. ''You
haven't earned my disapproval at all. What is more, I am
convinced that you will get what you want and what is right
for you.''

''Truly?'' she asked, gazing at him as though he were the
famous oracle at Delphi.

He patted her hand. ''Yes, truly.''

She believed him. Life was good once more and full of
infinite possibilities.

After she parted from him, she began thinking of some of
those possibilities. Then she began to consider how she
could turn possibilities into probabilities and probabilities
into sure success. As her old nurse had once told her, at the
same time she was praying to God, she should be swimming
away from the waterfall. In other words, she had to make
happen what she wanted to happen. Humming off-key, she
went to sit in a thick patch of grass to consider what she
should do.

The earl was not calm. He had received a very strange
note from Miss Hammond. She wanted him to meet her
alone in the gazebo on the hill. The word *alone* was
underlined three times. Why would she ask him to do that?

He considered not going, giving himself several excellent
reasons why he should not. Then he decided that he would
go, but only if accompanied by Lady Sanding. He needed to
spend more time with her, having invited her to Fairways
after all.

After being unable to locate Lady Sanding, who seemed
to have gone off with Mr. Hammond, he decided that he
would go to the gazebo by himself. He could not pass up the

opportunity to be alone with Miss Hammond. Perhaps he would even try again to kiss her.

On second thought, he wouldn't try; kissing her seemed to weaken his mind. He would simply meet her and find out what she wanted from him.

His route led him through a rose garden just beginning to show its buds, a topiary garden, and into the "ladies' garden," a pretty place verdant and juicy with new leaves and bright with the colors of early-spring flowers. It was there, to his surprise, that he found Regina Hammond.

"What are you doing here?" she asked, putting her hand to her lovely bosom as though he'd startled her.

"I might ask you the same thing. This was not where your note said I should find you."

"What note?"

The earl scowled. "Miss Hammond, please. I expected more from you."

Regina stared at him. "I do not understand. Why should you expect anything from me? And I did not send you a note."

"You signed it," he said, sounding irritated.

Regina backed away a little. "My lord, have you been imbibing?"

"Have *I* been imbibing? It was not I who sent you a note asking to meet you in the gazebo. What is it? Did you change your mind?"

"For the last time, my lord, I did not send you a note. Even if I had sent it, which I would not have done, I would not ask to meet you in a gazebo. Although you apparently do not have any regard for my reputation, I do. Why, if you dared to try to kiss me again, and we were to be found alone there, I could be forced to marry you."

There was a queer look in the earl's blue eyes. "You say that with such distaste, Miss Hammond. Would it be so bad if you were?"

"Of course it would be bad," she said with a frown. "I do not wish to marry you."

To Regina's surprise, the earl flushed. "I suppose you still want to marry my uncle," he said, his voice as hard as his expression. "You can put that out of your thoughts. I've already told you I will not permit such an event to take place."

Even though Regina did not care to marry Mr. James, it made her furious when the earl said that she would not be permitted to do so. "I'll marry him if I want to," she said between her teeth. "And neither you nor anyone else will be able to stop me."

"Won't we? Won't I? You are proposing a rough-and-tumble with the wrong person, Miss Hammond."

Regina gave a humorless laugh. "I do not wish to deal with you at all, my lord, whether roughly or smoothly. I do not wish to touch or even be in the same room with you. Get out of this garden, if you please; I was here first."

Lord Audlin drew himself up to his full, very impressive height. "The deuce I will. It is still *my* uncle's garden, dear, dear Miss Hammond," he said with a sneer. "It is not yet yours."

"Very well. Then I shall leave."

She made to do just that, but he grabbed her arm and would not let her go. "If you dislike me as much as you say, would you mind telling me before we part why you sent me that stupid note?"

"For the last time," she said, "I did not send you a note. Let me see it."

The earl took it from a pocket in his coattails and gave it to her. "That is not my handwriting," she announced triumphantly.

"You signed it."

"I did not. Not one single letter on this paper is in my handwriting, because it is not mine. It is . . . it is . . . oh, heavens."

He grabbed her shoulders. "What? Whose handwriting is it?"

"I don't care to tell you—I mean, I do not know."

"It must be Sarah Eckle's," he said with a sigh.

"Sarah?"

"Don't act as though you have no idea who that is, Miss Hammond. Sarah, Sally—your little friend." His eyes narrowed to blue slits. "Why would she sign your name to it?"

For answer, Regina blushed crimson.

"Do not change colors, Miss Hammond. You are not a chameleon. Speak."

Regina knew an order when she heard one. "She must have thought that you would more likely respond to a note from me than one from her. At least that is the only reason I can come up with."

The earl looked uncomfortable. "Why should she think that?" he asked in a low voice.

"I cannot imagine, my lord, since it should be obvious to anyone that you do not like me."

Instead of disclaiming such a feeling, he glared at her. Regina's head bent. Tiny little brown curls and thick ringlets fell forward, hiding her beautiful face. "What are you doing?" the earl demanded. He leaned forward and put a thumb under her chin. "Look at me, Regina."

Hesitantly she raised her head. Her brown eyes were huge and hurting. "I don't dislike you," the earl said.

"I don't believe you."

"I tell you I don't."

"Not even a little?"

"Not even a little. In truth . . ." The earl didn't finish his thought. He angled his head, said, "Regina, Regina," and slowly brought his mouth down to hers.

Regina heard a robin's song; she felt the sun's warmth on her muslin-clad shoulders; she smelled the intoxicating aromas of sweet, early flowers. If this were not paradise, it had to be a close approximation.

Then she was aware only of his lips on hers. They were hot. They were insistent and demanding. She opened her mouth and let his tongue come in.

She did not know exactly what the earl was offering, but she wanted it—all of it. She made a noise in the back of her throat. It was the sound of longing. The earl knew what it meant, and he let his kiss deepen.

His fingers ran through her hair, before his hands went to her shoulders and caressed them. Then they moved to her bosom and slipped under her blue fichu. He stroked the silky fullness there. Regina's breath caught in her throat and she choked.

Lord Audlin moved away from her. "I'm sorry," he said.

"At least that's more than you told me the last time you kissed me," Regina said wildly. Indeed, she looked wild with her heavy hair in disarray, her lips bright red and pouty.

"I'm sorry."

"Is that all you can say? You are a terrible man, my lord."

The earl sighed heavily. "You are right. Why can't I learn not to play with a child?"

The irate beauty slapped him.

The earl's right hand jerked, but he kept it at his side. His face was grim. "This will not happen again. I give you my word."

Regina focused her eyes on the ground, not wanting him to recognize that she still desired his lovemaking to go on—fool that she was. Without seeing it, she stared at the note that lay unheeded at his feet. Slowly the fog of passion that clouded her brain cleared. The note!

"My lord," she mumbled.

"Yes, Regina."

"My lord, you've forgotten the note."

"What note?" he asked, confirming her statement. "Oh, the note—the damn note. What are we going to do about it?"

We? she wanted to screech at him. We are not a we. We are two people who cannot make peace with each other. "I do not know," she said.

He put out his hand slowly. "Would you be willing to help me? I know I am not in your good graces, but this would be for your friend's sake."

The earl wasn't the only one who had a faulty memory. Once more Regina had forgotten about Sally and the loyalty she owed her. "I will," she said, "for my friend's sake."

"Good. Then I would like you to accompany me to the gazebo."

"And why should I do that—so that you can attack me again?"

The earl smiled at her remark. If his behavior could be considered an attack, he obviously knew that she had laid down her arms before it began. "I swear I will not attack you again," he said, his eyes twinkling. "Now, will you come?"

She glowered at him, but finally said, "Very well, but only because it is for Sally."

He extended his arm, and she put her hand on it. They walked thus, in silence, until they got to where they could see a charming white gazebo atop a small hill. A lone figure, her red hair brilliant in the light, sat there. She had a very large bosom, like that of a pouter pigeon. Despite the evidence of the red hair, for a moment Regina was uncertain as to who she was. No, it had to be Sally, although much inflated in the area of her chest, and she looked forlorn.

"She probably thought that I would have come here already," the earl said. Regina nodded.

Just then Sally looked in their direction. Her eyes widened at the sight of the earl and narrowed at the sight of Regina. "What are you doing here?" she asked her friend crossly.

"I . . . I was walking with the earl. It is a pleasant day for a walk."

Sally did not respond.

"He said that he got a note from me, but I told him that he did not. We do not know who could have sent it and used my name."

"I certainly don't know either," Sally said quickly. "I hope you don't believe I do."

Regina gave her a placating smile. "Of course we don't."

"It was probably Lady Sanding," Sally offered, switching her gaze to the earl's highly polished boots as though they were greatly fascinating.

"No doubt," said the earl. He came up to stand beside Sally. "It is a coincidence that you are here. Why are you?"

"Why?"

"Yes, that is what I asked. I am waiting for your answer."

She smiled at him weakly. "I don't know—that is, because it is a fine day, I decided to take a walk, and . . . and here I am."

"Indeed, you are. Where is Lady Sanding, I wonder, if it was she who sent me the note?"

Sally was beginning to appear ill. Regina thought she should tell Lord Audlin to stop tormenting her. On the other hand, Sally deserved some punishment for using Regina's name. Maybe she wouldn't say anything just yet.

"Have you finished interrogating me?" Sally cried. She stood up, her shoulders drooping. "For if you have . . ." She stopped speaking when she noticed the peculiar look in the earl's eyes. "What is it now?" she asked huffily, before following his glance down to her chest. "Oh."

Her posture had the unfortunate effect of emphasizing her incredible bosom. She crossed her arms over her bodice and looked daggers at the earl.

"Shall we all walk back to the house together?" Regina asked hastily.

Sally gave her a grateful smile. "That would be nice," she said. She observed the earl. Whatever she saw in his expression obviously discouraged her. "Thank you, but I don't believe I should quite yet. I . . . I am composing a poem. Yes, that is why I came here, and I need to be alone to do it."

The earl raised a dark eyebrow in a gesture of disbelief, but said nothing. Regina nodded.

Once more the earl offered Regina his arm. "Shall we go, Miss Hammond?"

They made to leave, but just as quickly stopped in their tracks. "Your mother is coming," Regina said. "Quick, do something."

Sally stared at her. "About what?"

Regina pointedly surveyed her friend's chest. "About your . . . your . . . you know."

The earl politely glanced away, although not before he was able to conceal his smirk. Sally turned as red as her hair, then whipped around and did something to her clothing. When she finally turned back, she was her slim, boyish self again.

The three of them watched Sally's mama come huffing and puffing up the hill. When she reached them, she eyed one, then another, confusion written clearly on her face, before she reached out toward her daughter. "Sarah, my dear child, are you all right?"

"Of course, Mama. Why wouldn't I be?"

"I don't know. Your note said that I was to come here at three o'clock to see something interesting. I am late because I only found the note at three." She glanced around with a puzzled smile. "What is interesting, dear?"

"It's the view, Mrs. Eckle," Regina said. "Isn't it lovely?" As she spoke she stole a peek at the earl. That was enough to reveal that he was furious.

"What is wrong?" she whispered.

His lips grim, Lord Audlin said, "That skinny chit meant to entrap me."

Regina opened her mouth to argue with him, but then closed it. She could see it clearly now: once Sally lured him to the gazebo, by using Regina's name, she meant to put herself in a compromising position, somehow. Then her mama would insist that the earl marry her daughter. Regina supposed that Sally's stuffed zona—whatever had she stuffed it with?—was to be used as bait to hold him there.

She had an urge to giggle, but another glance at Lord Audlin's face made her change her mind. No wonder he was angry.

"It's all right," she murmured to him while she resisted the impulse to stroke his arm in a mollifying way. "Nothing happened."

"No thanks to Miss Eckle," he murmured back. "Will you excuse us, ladies?" he said, taking Regina's hand and beginning to pull her. "Miss Hammond and I had made arrangements to walk with Mr. James."

The use of Mr. James's name had a very poor effect upon Sally. "I only did what he suggested," she said, her voice pitiful. "I did what he and my old nurse suggested. I swam away from the waterfall."

"Your friend is as mad as a hatter," the earl said out of the side of his mouth to Regina.

"She didn't used to be. I think that love has brought her low."

Lord Audlin gazed up at the heavens. "Spare me from the infatuations of children," he said in a religious tone of voice.

Was he talking about her? Regina opened her mouth to protest. Before she could say anything to him, however, he jerked her hand and pulled her down the hill. "Good-bye, Mrs. Eckle and Sally," she called over her shoulder, before she stopped speaking and started to run in order to keep the earl from dislocating her arm.

Once at the house, Lord Audlin abruptly excused himself. Leaving Regina standing just inside the door, he went off to look for the butler. When he located him, he said in an unconsciously threatening voice, "Where is Mr. James?"

Following the man's hastily given directions, he went to the library. His uncle was there, reading a book of love poems by Sappho. Seeing his nephew, he put down the book and smiled. The smile disappeared rather quickly, however.

"What is it, Steven?" he asked. "You look to be in a terrible state. Is something wrong?"

The earl sighted down his elegant nose at his uncle. "No, but it's no thanks to that bird-witted Miss Eckle—or to you, either, if she was speaking the truth."

Mr. James hastily rose out of his chair and stared at his nephew. "I do not know what you are talking about."

"Really? She gave me the impression that you would."

Mr. James tapped a booted foot nervously on the floor. "Well, I don't. Would you please explain yourself?"

The earl told Mr. James his story—neatly expurgated to leave out the part about his kissing Miss Hammond—and placed his hands aggressively on his hips. "What are you going to do about her?" he said.

"What am I going to do?" Mr. James asked. "What

makes you think I can do anything about her, or should?"

"Only the fact that she spends more time with you than with anyone else and that she brings up your name as though you were Socrates and Solon all in one."

"Is that so?" Mr. James seemed quite pleased by this information. "I didn't know that."

"You know it now. Will you talk to her?"

"I'm not her father," the earl's uncle said defensively, "no matter what she thinks."

"Of course, you are not. I wasn't suggesting that you were, especially not the way she looks at you."

Mr. James gazed at him as expectantly as a boy hoping he was about to receive a gift of toy soldiers. "How does she look at me?" he asked.

The earl slanted his head and stared at his uncle. "Why?"

"Why what?"

"Why do you want to know that?"

Mr. James shrugged and said casually, "Curiosity, I suppose. How does she look at me?" he repeated.

The earl thought for a moment. "She looks at you with respect."

"Oh? That is because she longs for a papa. She told me so."

"She also looks at you with tenderness."

"That's because—I don't know why. Do girls look at their papas like that?"

The earl shook his head. "I don't think so. I think the chit's starting to fall in love with you."

"With me?" Mr. James's face turned pink. "Is that so?"

"I may be wrong, of course, but I don't think so."

Mr. James seemed caught between delight and terror. "My goodness, what should I do? Do you think I need to borrow Lady Sanding for protection?"

"Certainly not. Would you mind if Miss Eckle were to decide she loves you rather than me?"

Instead of saying yes or no, Mr. James said, "She's a very nice girl. I'm quite fond of her."

"Are you? As fond as you are of Miss Hammond?"

Severn James looked annoyed. "Don't be ridiculous,

Steven. There is no comparison between them, so I could not possibly feel the same about them. Miss Eckle is adorable and sweet and fun. Do not make that face at me. She is. Miss Hammond, on the other hand, is . . .'' He groped for words. ''She is a goddess, and as such is to be worshipped.''

Worshipped, was it? The earl did not want to worship her. Doing so had never entered his mind. To him, she was a real flesh-and-blood female who smelled provocatively of heliotrope, not a goddess, and he wanted to treat her as such. He wanted to talk with her, joke with her, watch her whistle down birds. He wanted to roll to the bottom of hills with her and take her hand in his and run with her. He wanted to kiss her and let his fingers glide over her beautiful pale skin. And he wanted . . . Never mind!

He shook his head as though to clear it of intoxicating fumes. His thoughts were absurd. He didn't really want to do those things with her. She was a nuisance and a menace, to his uncle if not to him.

The earl sat and crossed his long legs. Thoughtfully he studied the tassel on his right boot. ''You still haven't told me if you'd mind being the object of Miss Eckle's affections,'' he said.

''What can I say? Miss Eckle is young. I am old enough to be her papa, which is probably why she thinks of me that way.''

The earl gave him a curious look. ''She is the same age as Miss Hammond. You didn't think you were too old for her.''

''I still do not, because the situation is different. Miss Hammond's beauty is such that it makes her seem ageless, or belonging to the ages, like a painting by da Vinci or—I don't know. I'm too surprised by what you said to think, Steven. I never expected this.''

''I don't know for certain that my observation is correct; I might be wrong.'' Mr. James's face fell. ''However, I do not think so. Perhaps we should send her home—send them both home.''

Now Mr. James looked like a boy whose toy soldiers

were in danger of being snatched away. "We will not. That would be . . . that would be rude. Yes. We will just have to let them continue here for a while until things sort themselves out."

The earl sighed. "As you wish. But you need to tell Miss Eckle to stop setting traps for me."

"I thought you said that she was developing a tendre for me." Mr. James sounded peevish.

"Yes, but I did not say that she knew she was. Obviously she still thinks she loves me. That's why she did what she did at the gazebo." He thought about her chest. "She's in a very confused state, I believe."

"I'll try to help her get through it," Mr. James said.

Was his uncle exchanging one sort of danger for another? If Sally Eckle needed him, he just might fall in love with her; he was that sort of a man.

Would that be so bad? For some reason, it did not bother the earl to think of his uncle being in love with Miss Eckle, and even marrying her.

There were other thoughts buzzing about in the earl's head, thoughts he did not wish to acknowledge. Unfortunately he could not rid himself of them. Since they all had to do with Regina Hammond, he felt angry with her. How dare she take over his mind? She was becoming a real nuisance. Whether his uncle wished it or not, it was important that she leave Fairways. And the sooner the better.

~Chapter 6

LORD AUDLIN WAS experiencing frustration. He wanted to talk to Miss Hammond and tried to do so the rest of that day. He did not get much of an opportunity, however, and at no time was he able to find her alone so that he could speak to her privately.

The earl had two reasons for wanting a tête à tête with her. One was that he felt he should thank her for protecting him from Sally's machinations. Directly after he got that over with, despite his uncle's objections he meant to suggest strongly that Regina return to London and take Sally Eckle with her. Of course, it went without saying that he would do it diplomatically.

The next morning he went searching for his quarry once more. Not locating her, he found himself becoming more and more irritated. How could he tell her to leave if he could not find her? Where was the vixen?

"Have you seen Miss Hammond?" he asked a passing maid.

The girl was carrying a feather duster. To his astonishment, she put the thing to her face, as though it were a gorgeous painted fan, then batted her eyelashes at him. What the devil did she think she was doing?

The earl sighed. Sometimes he felt he didn't like females at all. They were so . . . feminine. What normal person could understand them?

His expression must have made the girl decide she had better change her behavior. No longer coy, she said quickly, "I saw her go into the ballroom, Your Lordship."

"The ballroom! Why would she want to go there?"

"I'm sure I don't know, Your Lordship," she said, but it was doubtful that he heard her. He had already forgotten the maid's existence. He walked off, leaving her to stare admiringly at his broad-shouldered back and long, muscular legs encased in well-tailored buckskins.

The ballroom was an enormous pale green room containing six chandeliers swathed in dustcovers, six fireplaces, and gilt chairs too numerous to count; these latter were also swathed in dustcovers. Despite the room's size, Regina should have been easy to find—unless she, too, was under wraps.

The earl looked about, but did not see her. "Damnation," he said.

A sound caught his attention. It seemed to come from a far corner of the room, near a window heavily draped in green-and-gold brocade. He turned in that direction—and there she was, in all her glory.

As he closed in on her Regina gathered the skirts of her white muslin morning dress and hastily stood. "Good morning, my lord," she said with a notable lack of enthusiasm.

"So it is," the earl replied so coolly one would never suspect he'd felt a moment's annoyance. "Why are you hiding in here?"

Regina tilted her chin, very much the haughty young beauty. "I am not hiding. I . . . I was thinking."

The earl's blue eyes went over her, starting with the crown of her dark head and going to her peach-colored slippers, just peeking out of her gown. In between they lingered on her high bosom, tiny waist, and gently curving hips.

"May I ask of what you were thinking?"

In truth, she had been thinking about the earl's behavior toward her the previous day. After practically dragging her down the hill and then into the house following Sally's shameful actions, the earl had abandoned her and gone off to look for his uncle. It was not that she was used to men fawning over her—she wasn't even out yet and had very little experience with the opposite sex. Nevertheless he had kissed her a time or two or three, not that she was counting, and she expected more from him than to be brushed away as though she were a housefly.

"I do not believe I want to tell you, my lord," she finally said, wrinkling her smooth, pale brow.

"Good. I don't really want to know." Ignoring her peevish expression, he said, "I came looking for you to thank you for your help yesterday. It would have been bellows to mend for me if you had not been with me."

Regina blushed rosily. "I did not do anything. I was just there."

"I'm glad you were," the earl said with a smile.

Regina looked troubled. "Sally didn't mean anything by what she did," she said. "Sometimes she becomes . . . um, overly enthusiastic about her ideas."

"Perhaps so," Lord Audlin said with a look that told her he did not believe her. "Nevertheless her mama surely would have meant something. If not for you, I might have found myself affianced to your bird-witted friend."

Regina found that the thought horrified her. Her lips thinned and she frowned at the earl.

Assuming that she objected to his choice of adjectives, he said more mildly, "She is bird-witted, you know. That is why I need your help once more."

"My help? To accomplish what, my lord?"

Instead of answering, he stared at her face, forgetting what had been on his mind. Why did Regina have to be so beautiful? he thought. Why, especially, did she have to be so beautiful in that particular combination of skin and hair and facial features? And why did he have to find her provoking behavior so fascinating? He had known many stunning women, but only Regina Hammond's looks and nature left him feeling vulnerable. He did not bless her for her effect on him.

"Why do you need my help?" Regina asked again, more to make him cease looking at her in such a disturbing way than anything else. When still he did not answer, she said,

"Do you want me to promise that I will not marry your uncle? Is that it, my lord?"

He shook his head as though coming out of a spell, then said, "Would you?"

"No, I would not."

"I did not think you would. That is why I will not ask you to."

Regina was disappointed. Didn't he care? She would not like it if he did not.

"I want you to help me with your friend Sally, Miss Hammond. Even you must admit that she's becoming a menace."

In truth, Regina could not deny it—although she would to her last breath. "Ummm," she said noncommittally.

He raised a dark eyebrow. "What do you think we should do to discourage her?"

We? Did he really expect her to help him in that way? If he did, he'd made a mistake. "Why don't you ask Lady Sanding for assistance?" she said curtly.

Lord Audlin almost said, "Who?" but stopped himself in time. "Lady Sanding seems occupied with other things lately."

Regina looked worried. "Yes, she does, doesn't she?"

The earl's stare was penetrating. "What are you saying?"

"I am saying the same thing you are," she replied, sounding cross. "I believe that she and my papa are becoming . . . uh . . . quite friendly."

"Oh-ho. Don't tell me you'd mind if she and your father developed a tendre for each other."

"Tendre?" she said bitterly. "Don't be ridiculous."

Lord Audlin put his hands on his lean hips. "What does that mean?"

"He's my papa. He doesn't develop tendres."

The earl laughed. "It is you who are being ridiculous, I'm afraid. Men do, even men who are papas. You must be very young, indeed, Miss Hammond, not to know that."

Regina raised her hand as though she wanted to strike him.

"Don't even think of it," he said in a tone that sent shivers down her spine.

She lowered her hand but said defiantly, "He still loves my mama, even though she is dead. He even talks to her sometimes."

The earl looked disapproving, started to say something, then clamped his lips together.

"Well?" Regina said, making the one word sound like a challenge. "Will you ask Lady Sanding to help you?"

"No. I am asking you." He pulled two gilt chairs over to him and undid their covers. "Sit down, Miss Hammond. I am tired of standing."

Reluctantly she did as she'd been bid. "I want to request something of you," he said. "Do you think it is possible for us to be, if not friends, at least allies?"

Regina was still in a snit thinking about her papa and Lady Sanding. Wasn't it enough that Her Ladyship had captured the earl's heart? Did she have to have Regina's papa's heart as well? "I don't think so," she said.

"Well, that is plain speaking. Miss Hammond . . . ?"

"Another question, my lord?"

"No. Please go home, Miss Hammond, back to London, and take your friend with you."

Regina's expression became regally cold. "I don't think I'll do that, my lord. Rather I'll stay here awhile longer. I find the country so pleasant this time of year. And so does Miss Eckle."

What the earl did not know—at least, she hoped he did not—was that she had no reason to return to London. Her papa was still in no position to pay for a season for her. What would she do in London?

For a moment her dark, beautiful eyes filled with tears of self-pity. However, she refused to succumb to the dismals. Many people had far worse problems than she. She was not acquainted with any of them, but still she was certain there must be such people. She shook her head as though to emphasize her rejection of Lord Audlin's command.

The earl's smile was sly. "Won't you leave even to save your father from the exquisite paws of Lady Sanding?"

Regina bit at her lower lip. "I . . . don't know. I will have to think about that."

Victory might be near, he thought, and wondered why the idea did not give him any pleasure. What he said was, "What is there to think about, Miss Hammond?"

For the first time her voice became a bit shrill. "There is the fact that you'll say anything to make me go away. Tell me, my lord, can you not learn to tolerate me? Is that asking so much?"

The earl looked shocked. "Tolerate . . . ?" Did one merely tolerate a stunning sunset? A harvest moon? A sky thick with shining stars? One did not tolerate beauty; one reveled in it and thanked the Lord for it.

He put out his hand to her, but slowly dropped it. It was as though he didn't know what to do, didn't have any acceptable choices, was all adrift and in imminent danger of drowning.

He rose, gazed down at her, and then, without another word, turned on his heel and left the room.

Regina stared after him. Everything was his fault, she thought indiscriminately—her semiofficial engagement, Sally's bizarre behavior, her father's burgeoning tendre for Lady Sanding, everything! If only she could do something to make Lord Audlin leave Fairways instead of her. Surely each of the guests there would be the better for it, even he. What she needed was a plan.

"Ah, Steven, what are you doing up here?" This greeting, delivered in an abstracted way, was from Mr. James, who was standing outside the door of the ballroom.

"Nothing," the earl answered as casually as though he had not just gone through a bad experience. He was not about to tell his uncle what had transpired. Indeed, he was not about to tell him that the fair Regina was sitting alone in the ballroom, even if it was his uncle's ballroom.

Mr. James shifted a piece of statuary he'd been staring at from his left hand to his right and put his free hand on his nephew's sleeve. "I was looking for you," he said.

The earl's eyes narrowed in puzzlement. Why, if his

uncle had been surprised to see him in that part of the house, had he been looking for him there? It was better not to ask, he decided. "I am at your service, Uncle."

"Good, good. What did you have in mind for entertaining our guests today, especially Miss Hammond and Miss Eckle?"

If the earl told him what he had in mind, his uncle would never speak to him again. "I have not thought of anything," he said untruthfully.

"Could you try? I'd hate to see Miss Hammond—I mean, any of our guests become bored and restless."

"Very well. Let us go to the library, if you will, and discuss it."

Once there, the two men settled into comfortable leather chairs. The earl stretched out his long legs and stared at the toe of his right boot as though it held the answer to his uncle's queries. Perhaps it did, because shortly he said, "I might have an idea or two."

"Wonderful," Mr. James said enthusiastically, then added in a more cautious tone, "I hope that nothing you think of is too active, like riding, or sliding down hills, or shooting arrows. Our guests, you know—we need to think of them."

"But, Uncle, the girls enjoyed doing those things, and you did say before that you did not want them to become bored and restless. Do not tell me that you have no further wish to entertain them." His uncle looked at him mutely. The earl added in a hopeful voice, "Do not tell me that you've tired of Miss Hammond and Miss Eckle already."

Mr. James flushed. "Certainly I have not, especially of Miss Hammond. It is simply that I have no desire to get dirty today. Your ideas do not concern things that will cause us to get dirty, do they?"

The earl tapped a finger against his chin. "Let me see," he said. "We need something that will not cause us to get dirty but will keep the children busy. Also, it should not be too strenuous."

"I did not mention a word about strenuousness," Mr. James protested.

Lord Audlin smiled at his uncle affectionately. "Indeed, you did not. I was thinking out loud."

"Naturally I would not mind if it were something quieter, something which would even allow me to read for a while. I have started the most wonderful book, Steven. . . . Well, never mind. I suppose it will keep until later."

"Um, something that is clean, will keep the children busy, is not strenuous, is quiet, and affords one a chance to read. I think, perhaps, we should all climb into bed together."

"Steven!"

The earl grinned, his temper much improved. "No? Then let me think." He walked about in a circle upon the fine red-and-blue Turkey carpet, his head bent. After a few minutes he stopped and said, "I have it. We must go on a picnic."

"A picnic?" Mr. James looked doubtful. "I haven't been on a picnic in years. Are you certain that all of our guests will enjoy that?"

"They had better," the earl said arrogantly.

"Very well. Where shall we have the picnic?"

Lord Audlin thought a minute, then said, "Let us go to one of the streams off the Medway. We can take fishing poles with us in case anyone wants to fish."

Mr. James nodded. "I'll tell Cook to prepare a lunch. Why do you not apprise the others of our plans?"

The earl agreed, and the two men went off.

His Lordship found all the guests, including Regina, in the music room. Lady Sanding was playing a merry piece on the pianoforte while Mr. Hammond stood nearby, ready to turn the pages for her. The rest of the group sat on gilt chairs very similar to those in the ballroom. Except for Regina, who frowned at the couple at the pianoforte, everyone seemed to be enjoying the entertainment.

When he came in, Her Ladyship stopped playing and turned to him. "Steven," she said in a low, intimate-sounding voice, which caused Mr. Hammond to frown as severely as his daughter. Lady Sanding put out her hand.

The earl kissed it.

"I missed you," she said.

At this remark, the two Hammonds looked absolutely murderous. Sally Eckle, on the other hand, appeared indifferent.

The earl decided not to comment upon Lady Sanding's words. There was no need to add insult to injury. "I came to tell everyone that we are to go on a picnic."

"A picnic?" the various voices echoed.

"Yes. Are there any objections?"

Regina felt the urge to object, just to be contrary. "I'm not going," she said, the line of her mouth tense and willful.

"Not going? Oh, but you should." This was from Lady Sanding.

"You most certainly are going, young lady," said her papa, who, ordinarily, did not much mind what she did or didn't do as long as it wasn't scandalous and didn't interfere with his card playing. What was wrong with him?

"Very well," Regina said in a grumpy voice.

"Is it hot outside? I might not go myself if it is hot," Lady Sanding declared, already looking limp.

The earl smiled gently at her. "Are you afraid you might melt?" he asked.

He never smiled at *her* like that, Regina fumed. If only the sun would blaze as though this were Africa instead of England and Lady Sanding would refuse to leave the house.

Regina was not in luck. Assured by all the men that she would be fanned vigorously if she gave even the tiniest hint of wilting, Her Ladyship agreed to go.

The only one who refused to go and could not be persuaded to change her mind was Mrs. Eckle. She had made plans to write down some of Cook's excellent recipes, she said, and did not mean to alter her plans.

As for Sally, she seemed beside herself with delight, her mama's disinclination to accompany them and her embarrassment over the previous day's fiasco with the earl notwithstanding. She clapped her hands as though she were truly the child the earl thought her, then urged Regina to run up to their bedroom with her to change into something more appropriate for dining al fresco.

"You must wear your yellow," Sally said when she shut the bedroom door after them. "You look like a daisy in it with your dark hair and eyes." Not waiting for Regina's response, she pulled the yellow muslin gown from the wardrobe and tossed it to the bed.

"I suppose I'll have to wear white," she continued sadly. "No other color suits me."

"You may borrow my green silk sash and green bonnet and parasol," Regina offered generously. "Green suits you very well."

"Thank you," Sally said gratefully. "You are very good to me."

Regina thought that perhaps she did not deserve to be called good, but at least she could have been worse. She could have "helped" the earl with his plans. She gave her friend only a half-guilty smile.

A mere three quarters of an hour later the two young ladies joined the others in the entrance hall. Soon all those who were going on the outing were deposited in a coach or were on horseback, and off they went, followed by a wagon containing rugs, blankets, and baskets of good-smelling food.

Since the River Medway flowed past Tonbridge, the party went through the market town to reach their destination. It was the girls' first glimpse of Tonbridge, and they were pleased with what they saw. They were even more pleased when they arrived at a grassy area near the river shaded by large willow trees and sweet with the odor of honeysuckle.

The servants put down the rugs and blankets, and the guests settled themselves. "Shall we eat now?" Mr. James asked with a worried look, his duties as host apparently weighing heavily on his mind.

"We've only just got here," Sally replied indignantly. "We should engage in some sort of activity before we eat."

"Activity?" Mr. James sounded doubtful. "What sort of activity?"

"I don't know. Perhaps we could play a game."

Lady Sanding smiled provocatively in Mr. Hammond's direction. "I don't play games, at least not of that sort."

"There's the stream over there," Regina said abruptly. "Let us go to look at it."

"I suppose you like streams because they attract birds and other creatures," said Mr. James.

"That is a good reason," she agreed. She flashed him a smile that caused more than its recipient to catch his breath.

The stream along which they were situated was very pleasant, and looked as though it would be a good spot for fishing. "I know," said Sally, who had given it no more than a cursory glance. "We must play ducks and drakes."

Mr. James groaned. "Must we? I have not played that since I was a child, and I am certain I will be no good at it."

"Of course you will," Sally told him in a bracing voice. She picked up a flat stone from the ground. "Look, here's a perfect stone. Go ahead; try your luck."

"Luck it will be," replied Mr. James, but he accepted the stone and threw it toward the water, where it promptly sank. Since the object of the game was to see how many times one could skip it along the river's surface before it disappeared, Mr. James had not done well at all.

"You'll be much better on your next try," Sally said consolingly. He gave her a grateful look.

It was Regina's turn next. "I'd like to practice first," she said.

The earl gave her an indulgent male smile. "Certainly."

Regina's first few efforts were as bad as Mr. James's. The earl's smile broadened. She looked up at him and said, "Let this time count." With limber wrist, she threw the stone. It skipped three times before disappearing.

The earl looked at her suspiciously, but she seemed all innocence. Somehow, however, he had a feeling that he had been hoaxed. "Lady Sanding?" he said, procuring another stone.

"Not I, my dear."

"Nor I," said Mr. Hammond.

"Very well. Then I shall take my turn." With a graceful motion, the earl released the stone. It skimmed across the water, skipping three times. Regina and the earl were tied.

For the next hour the two continued grimly to throw stones while the other people drifted away. "Look at that," Regina crowed after her last turn. "My stone skipped four times. Do you concede defeat, my lord?"

The earl eyed her stubbornly. "I never concede defeat, Miss Hammond. We Earls of Audlin don't. In fact, the family's motto is, 'Ever onward, and never admit defeat.' I've taken that to heart."

"My stone skipped four times," Regina repeated, looking as stubborn as he.

Instead of replying, the earl selected a smooth, stream-worn stone and sent it sailing over the water. It skipped five times.

"I do not wish to play anymore," Regina said, both her temper and her color high. She stamped her foot, then flung herself around and scampered back to the others as rapidly as she could.

By this time the group on the blankets had finished their meal and were sitting and lying about in various attitudes. Sally was near to Mr. James, a little way off from Lady Sanding and Mr. Hammond. With apparent delight she was listening to him read from a book of poetry.

"You read so well," she said admiringly when he paused to turn a page. "I wish I could read like that."

The earl made a snorting noise.

For an instant Mr. James looked as though he would like to kill the earl in some inventive, horrible way. However, when Sally put her hand on his arm, he subsided without saying a word.

Perhaps it was Sally Mr. James should be courting, Regina thought. There was a rapport between them that was obvious. She turned to look at the earl to share this revelation with him, but then she changed her mind. He was not her friend.

"Hello, daughter," her papa boomed. "Did you have a good time with your game?"

Why was he looking so happy? Regina thought sourly. And why was he so close to Lady Sanding? One little wiggle and his head would be in her lap. "Are you tired, Papa?" she said, pretending to a solicitude she did not feel; to say the truth, she was furious. "Perhaps we should return to Fairways so that you can rest."

"Rest," her papa repeated as though the word were in Urdu or Welsh or some other incomprehensible tongue. "Nothing of the sort. I never felt more full of spirit in my life."

Lady Sanding giggled and looked with approval at Mr. Hammond.

Regina sat down next to them. "My papa loves cards," she told Lady Sanding in a low voice, apparently apropos of nothing.

Lady Sanding smiled at Regina. "Yes, I discovered that."

"He likes to gamble," Regina volunteered.

Her Ladyship nodded her beautiful head. "Who does not?"

Regina was feeling desperate. "Unfortunately he loses. He loses a lot."

"Yes, it's such fun to do that."

Regina stared at her uncomprehendingly.

"That is because it does not matter," Her Ladyship continued cheerfully. "My dear husband left me so much money that I could lose at cards practically forever and it would not make an iota of difference."

Losing made quite a difference to Mr. Hammond, but Regina, as much as she wanted to discourage Lady Sanding from forming an attachment to him, could hardly say that. Besides, she had the feeling that such information would not discourage the woman. She would probably announce what fun it was to care about one's losses.

Regina rose to her feet. "If you'll excuse me," she said.

The earl's hand came out and clamped around her wrist. "Do not go away. You have not eaten anything."

She attempted to free her hand, but he would not allow it. "I am not hungry," she said proudly.

"Sit, and eat." He accompanied his words by putting pressure on her wrist.

Unless she wanted to go about with her arm in a sling, there was nothing for Regina to do but obey him. With bad grace, she sank to her knees. The earl came down beside her. "Pickle?" he asked.

How she wished she could rub it over his cheeks and under his elegant nose. "No!"

"Some ham? Chicken?"

"My lord, I can help myself!"

"Then do so," he said, speaking low, "and do not spoil everyone else's good time."

She had to admit to herself that what he said was just. She grabbed up a piece of pickle and stuck it in her mouth, unfortunately choking on the juice. Grinning, the earl pounded her back.

Revenge! She had to get revenge, if not this day then later. In the meantime she would settle for putting some distance between them. After eating several morsels of untasted food as quickly as she decently could, she announced that she had had sufficient and rose to her feet. "I am going fishing," she said, grabbing a fishing pole that had been placed against a tree. "Please, don't anyone join me. That would scare away the fish."

When she looked over her shoulder and saw that the earl had made no move to follow her, she felt a surge of disappointment. It made her want to cry. Whatever was the matter with her?

She glanced down at the pole and saw that someone had put a worm on the end of it. Poor worm. She did not know what to do about it. If she did not attempt to fish and the earl came after her, heaven forfend, he might think that she was trying to keep away from him because he'd bested her at ducks and drakes—which would be no more than the truth. "I'm sorry," she whispered to the worm before casting the line into the water.

Fifteen minutes later she was still standing there, waiting for she did not know what, never having fished before. "Pull it in," the earl's excited voice suddenly called out behind her. "Damn it, Regina, there's something on your line. Pull it in."

"You cursed at me," she said haughtily, "and I did not give you permission to call me Regina."

"I'll apologize later. Give me that line." He pressed himself against her and put his arms around her, grabbing the pole just below where she held it. Then he gave a tug. A short while later he brought in a fish.

"Look at that," he said as proudly as though he had spawned the creature himself. "That's grand. Isn't it, Regina? Regina, what is the matter? You aren't going to get upset over this fish, are you?"

"Poor fish," she said. "It can't breathe. Put it back."

"Back?" The earl was outraged. "I most certainly will not. That's my fish."

The gasping fish was now off the hook. There was only one way to save him. With a look of terrified resolution, Regina gave the earl a push. As he landed in the stream she sent the fish sailing over his head. Waiting for nothing, it swam away.

The earl came up sputtering. "At your old tricks again, are you?" he said, before lunging forward and grabbing her ankle. The next thing Regina knew, she was in the water beside him.

A wet, sputtering young beauty pulled her head from the water. The earl looked at her expectantly. "You," she said before scooping her hand over the stream's surface and splashing him. Then she burst into laughter.

The earl looked vastly pleased but astonished. "Don't you mind that you are wet?" he asked.

Still crouching, Regina shook her head. "No. Should I mind?"

"But your hair is wet. Females don't like to get their hair wet, especially when they are in company."

"Don't they? I don't care," she said, laughing again. "The sun will cause it to dry." With a careless push of her fingers, she moved the tangle of heavy curls back from her glowing face.

The earl put out his hands to help her stand. "You aren't in the least enamored of your looks, are you?" he said with grudging admiration.

"Enamored? What do you mean? Do you expect me to be in love with myself?" She ended her sentence with a giggle.

This time there was no like response from the earl. Indeed, he seemed struck dumb. That was because he could finally see her clearly—very clearly: the dunking had plastered her now nearly transparent gown against her body. He could even see where her nipples were; the water had made them harden and thrust against the cloth that covered her breasts.

He gulped. "You are . . . you are . . . beautiful, Regina," he said in a low, emotion-laden voice, "even more beautiful than I had imagined. Perhaps you are not enamored of yourself, but . . ." He did not finish his sentence. Instead one big hand came out and slowly stroked her arm.

Regina shivered.

"You're cold," he said.

She started to protest that she was not, but by then he had pulled her into his arms, and the protest died on her lips.

He held her tight against his body inside his coat. "Are you warmer now?" he asked in a not quite steady voice.

Warmer? Yes, she was warmer, despite his being as wet as she. Indeed, Regina felt that like the phoenix, she might spontaneously experience combustion and go up in flames.

~Chapter 7

REGINA WAS FULLY aware, however, that unlike the phoenix, if she went up in flames, she wouldn't be reborn all nice and new. "You'd best let me go," she said not without a struggle. She gazed into his blue eyes. They looked as lazy and sleepy as a cat's—yet very dangerous. "Now please," she added with a frightened gulp.

Once more the earl was the cool, sophisticated lord she was used to dealing with. "So I'd better."

He helped her up onto the bank, then shed his gray coat and put it around her. "Do not take this off," he said.

"But it is wet."

"That doesn't matter. Don't argue with me, Regina. Trust me, and leave it on."

She could not help herself; the smile she gave him was cynical. Trust him? She might seem a child to him, but she wasn't a complete fool.

The earl flushed. Amazingly she had hurt his feelings. She would never have imagined that she, or anyone else, could do that to him.

"Don't you know why I want you to wear my coat?" he said angrily. "Do you think it is because I want to keep you warm and safe? I'd as soon attempt to protect a lioness."

Regina's lush mouth tightened momentarily. "Well then, why?"

"I did not want you to suffer embarrassment. Now that your gown is wet, it reveals . . . um . . . more of your charms than is seemly."

Regina's blush was so intense, it seemed as though it had

to be painful, like a burn. "Thank you," she said stiffly, and jerked the coat harder around herself. Almost running, she made certain she stayed ahead of him.

"There you are," said her papa as she came up to the four remaining picnickers. "Did you fall in the water?" Regina nodded. "And the earl lent you his coat; that was kind."

The others made murmuring sounds apparently meant to signify that they were paying attention to the conversation. In truth, however, none of them seemed very interested in Regina or the earl. Her papa and Lady Sanding had been playing piquet, Regina noticed, and from their expressions were eager to resume their game. As for Sally and Mr. James, he still had his book in his hand and must have been reading to her the whole time Regina was dallying with the earl at the stream.

Lady Sanding raised her blond head. "You're wet, Miss Hammond. Why is that?" she asked in surprise, thus providing proof of Regina's belief that she had not been listening.

Mr. James looked up then, too. "My heavens, Miss Hammond, you *are* wet. And so are you, Steven."

Regina gazed at the lot of them with disgust.

"No harm done," the earl said as though nothing that mattered had happened. "Miss Hammond fell in the stream, but I pulled her out almost immediately. She'll be fine."

Regina's mouth tightened mutinously. It was easy for the earl to make up stories and gloss over matters; he was untouched by what had transpired. Not she, however. For a few minutes she had felt his approval; they had been friends and liked each other. Then that other feeling had taken over—and now she wasn't convinced she'd ever be fine again.

Wasn't it Shakespeare or someone like that who had written about a person suffering a sea change? If she asked Mr. James, he would be able to identify the author. Not that it signified. She knew she had suffered a stream change and was different somehow.

It seemed to Regina that everyone at the picnic was different, except the earl, of course. If one did not know better, one would think that not only were the two couples on the blankets perfectly paired, like a superb team of matched horses, but that they knew it and reveled in the knowledge. Only she and the earl seemed out of step.

"I want to go home," she said, feeling deeply depressed by her observations. "I don't wish to be here anymore."

"I do hope you mean Fairways," her papa said unfeelingly, "for we shan't be leaving for London today."

Mr. James nodded. "Of course she does. I wouldn't hear of anything else."

The earl looked at Regina. Whatever he saw galvanized him into immediate action. "Miss Eckle, walk your friend to the carriage," he said in a commanding voice. "The rest of you get ready to leave. I shall instruct the servants to collect the picnic things and follow."

Everyone did as he'd been bid and soon Regina was seated in the comfortable carriage, on her way back to Fairways, dry clothing, a warm bed, and a sedative medicine to help her sink into sleep and get over her loss of composure.

She slept through dinner and, in fact, did not get up until the following morning. Physically she felt quite well, but concerning her feelings—in truth, if she did not manage to avoid the earl from that time on, she did not know what she'd do. The excess of strong emotion he generated in her made her uncharacteristically nervous and irritable. It made her want to get away from the other guests, especially the earl.

"I want to go to Tunbridge Wells today," she announced to Mr. James and her papa after she joined them for breakfast. "Can we do that?"

Mr. James nodded his head. "Certainly, my dear. I will just find Miss Eckle and the others and ask them along."

"No," she said in a panic-filled voice. "I mean, no. I want to go with just the two of you."

"Oh, but Miss Eckle—"

"We should ask Lady Sanding," Mr. Hammond interrupted his host.

Regina's face was a mask of unhappiness. "I don't want to," she said with a quaver in her voice.

"Are you sure you feel all right?" her papa asked. "Not coming down with a cold or an ague?" Regina shook her head. "Oh, very well. Just the three of us will go. Won't we, James?"

"Certainly," replied Mr. James, although his tone lacked enthusiasm.

Not more than a half hour later they left the house, telling no one except the butler where they were going. The carriage took them past pretty black-and-white-timbered farmhouses, orchards filled with fruit trees, and fields planted with row upon row of corn and other vegetables. The air coming into the coach was sweet with the smell of fruit blossoms and wild honeysuckle. If Regina had been in a better state of mind, she would have enjoyed herself immensely.

But she was not in a better state of mind. The trip, thus far, had not done anything to alleviate her dark mood. She stared out the window, saying nothing, until they reached Tunbridge Wells and were set down by the coachman at Bath Square.

"Perhaps you should have a cup of the waters," Mr. Hammond said with a worried glance at his child. "You're looking peaked and are probably in need of a restorative."

Regina shook her head. "No, I'm not. I'd rather shop."

The men blanched, but gallantly lined up on either side of her to walk in the shade of the lime trees along the colonnade, which was paved with the famous Princess Anne pantiles. Regina peered intently into each of the stores in the arcade. "I want to go in that one," she said, beginning to enjoy herself, her mind occupied finally with more pleasant thoughts.

"Of course," both men agreed in unison.

She almost laughed at their eagerness to cheer her, but managed to control herself and entered a pretty sort of shop filled with pagoda-shaped parasols, umbrellas of every description, and assorted reticules and gloves.

"It is too bad Miss Eckle is not here," Mr. James

murmured. "I am sure she would like to look at these parasols." He turned uncertainly toward Regina. "Would it be improper of me to purchase one for her, do you think?"

Before she could reply, Mr. Hammond said, "So would Lady Sanding enjoy this shop. What a pity she is missing it. Regina, would it be amiss if I got that white parasol with the ebony handle for her? Or would the gesture be too . . . too . . . ?"

"It would definitely be too-too," she said jealously, still being unused to having to share her father. "Besides, zebras do not need parasols."

"Zebras? Why what do you mean?" He gave her a fulminating look. "Are you calling Lady Sanding a zebra?"

"I believe she is," Mr. James said, appearing dumbfounded. Then he put his hand over his mouth and muttered behind it, "Tell me, Hammond, is Miss Hammond often like this?"

"Like what?"

"I don't know . . . sort of snappish and unpleasant."

"Of course not. You've seen her." He stared at Mr. James with wrinkled forehead and narrowed eyes. "What is it, James? Are you changing your mind about wanting to marry her?"

"Marry *her*?" Mr. James asked as though he'd never considered the idea. He added hastily, "No, no, certainly I am not changing my mind. How could you think it?"

"May I know what you are talking about?" Regina asked a bit more mildly than before, having been rather intimidated by her usually indulgent papa's tone.

Although neither man supplied an answer, she thought with displeasure that she knew the subject of their conversation. Either her papa was discussing Lady Sanding or Mr. James was talking about Sally. She did not mind much about the latter, though her suitor's defection could not help but rankle just a bit. It was the former that concerned her.

She wondered if her papa and Mr. James were aware of their predilection for the two ladies. She would not wager on her papa not knowing, but it would not surprise her if Mr. James were unaware. There seemed to be so much that escaped his notice—like her burgeoning feelings for the earl. But she would not think about that.

However, the choice was not to remain hers. It was scarcely an hour later, as they were leaving another shop, that they came upon the rest of the house party. Regina noticed that the earl, who was holding a parcel, was walking quite close to Lady Sanding. Had he bought his mistress a present? Once again, Regina experienced jealousy. She could not help herself.

Mr. Hammond interrupted her thoughts by pushing her out of the way. "My dear Lady Sanding," he said, "how glad I am to see you. How did you know we were here?"

She smiled and patted his hand. "If by 'here' you mean Tunbridge Wells, the butler told us it was your destination."

Looking satisfied, Mr. Hammond nodded. "We were examining some parasols in a shop when I said that one of them would exactly suit you. Naturally, it was black and white. Would you care to see it?"

Her Ladyship's desires in that direction were quickly made obvious. Leaving the earl without a by-your-leave, Lady Sanding practically shoved Mr. Hammond down the arcade.

"There was a very nice parasol there for you, too," Mr. James said shyly to Sally. He looked at her mama. "Oh, yes, and one you would like as well. Would you care to see them?" he asked.

Mrs. Eckle nodded, then looked at Regina, who could guess that Sally's mama did not want her to stand outside alone with the earl. However, despite herself, that was what Regina wanted to do. She turned her back on Mrs. Eckle and pretended to be unaware when the older woman and the others walked off.

The earl gazed at her. "I missed you this morning, Regina."

"Oh, really?" She made her voice sound bored.

The earl took her stubborn chin in his fingers. "Look at me," he said.

Regina reluctantly raised her eyes to his face.

"What is it?"

"What is what?" she said, pretending not to understand his question.

For just a second the earl appeared irritated. Then in a voice so sympathetic it surprised her, he said, "What is wrong? Did you catch a chill yesterday?"

Regina shook her head. Her lips pursed.

"Do you feel unwell in some other way?"

Again she shook her head without answering.

"Are you suffering from melancholia?"

Instead of shaking her head this time, Regina sniffed and looked away. She could hardly tell him that he was the cause of her unhappiness.

"See here," he said in a voice meant to comfort and soothe, "I bought you something."

Regina still did not look at him. "Why?" she said in a voice almost too low to be heard.

"Why?" he repeated. In truth, he'd asked himself that very question. The answer was that he couldn't stop himself from doing it. You'd better by wary, Audlin, he told himself. You'll end up in parson's mousetrap—with the merry little mouse calling the tune.

Apparently Regina had decided that he did not mean to answer her question. "What is it?" she asked.

He almost said, What is what? but caught himself. "I'd like you to guess."

She started to refuse, but he looked so earnest and worried, unlike anything she'd seen in him heretofore, that she did not have the heart to reject his game. She studied the brown-paper-wrapped oblong. "It is a dead pheasant," she said with a reluctant smile, "to go with the one that fell out of the tree when you whistled it down."

The earl grinned. My, he was attractive. Regina gazed admiringly at the way his fine blue coat fit over his broad shoulders. He had very well-shaped, long legs, also. She'd noticed that. She always noticed it. The observation excited her every time, too. "Guess again," he said.

Regina came out of her reverie. "Um . . . it's a container of worms so that I can catch another fish and you can act like a gloating savage over it once again."

The earl put back his head and laughed. As he did so, Regina looked up into his mouth. Why, he still had all of his teeth, and at his age, too. She sighed.

"You have one more chance to guess it," the earl said with mock sternness. "If you don't, I might not let you have your gift."

Regina's comely face grew mock serious. She bent her head, studying the rather small package in his hand. "It's my own private hill, for me to roll down anytime I want."

"Only if you let me accompany you," he said in a husky voice.

Regina turned her hands palms up in a gesture of confusion. "My lord, I fear I do not understand you. I feel as though you want something from me, but I do not know what it is."

"What do I want?" The elegant bones in his face became more prominent as he spoke. "I want to want nothing from you, but that doesn't seem to have any effect on my desires. I'm afraid I want everything you have to give, Regina—or that I can take. I want your brown eyes and your silky skin. I want your pretty neck and your white shoulders. I want your lips. And I want other things, like your laughter and spirit and—"

She stood on tiptoe and clamped her hand over his mouth. "Stop it," she said before releasing his mouth.

"I wish I could. Regina, my love, what am I going to do with you?"

His hands went around her arms and tightened on them. His eyes were very bright and fixed on her face. He frightened her. "Nothing," she said shrilly. "You'll do nothing with me. I won't let you."

It was as though she had thrown cold water on him. He shrugged and said in a voice devoid of emotion, "Then I suppose I got you the right thing. Here, Miss Hammond."

Regina put out her hand and accepted the package. She tore off the paper wrapping with nervous, eager fingers, then gazed inside. What she saw was a beautiful doll with wide brown eyes and thick, curly hair of the same dark color. It looked amazingly like her. "Play with this," he said, "and don't bother me anymore."

"Bother you?" she said sharply. "It was you who asked me to indulge you in your silly game."

The earl's expression became stern. "Is that so?"

Regina nodded forcefully, causing her rich brown curls to bob. The earl reached out his hand, then pulled it back. "Everyone makes a mistake now and then," he said. "Mine was in treating you like a woman rather than a girl. I won't do it again." With that, he went after the others, into the parasol shop, leaving her outside alone.

"Won't do it again," she repeated to herself. He had withdrawn from her—leaving her with a sense of having been deprived of sunlight, warmth, and nourishment. She looked down at the baby doll. It stared back with its huge eyes. She fancied it was asking her why she had behaved as she did with the earl.

"I can't help it," she muttered. "He makes me feel as though I don't know who I am."

To be perfectly honest, he did more than that to her. He made her experience envy when he devoted himself to others, such as to Lady Sanding. He made her miss him when he was not there. He made the world bright when he was nice to her. And he made her long for the feel of his mouth slanting over hers and the touch of his hands on her skin.

She had to stop thinking about him; it was too upsetting. She walked down to the shop to join the others but stopped outside the door when she saw that they were all trooping out—Sally and Lady Sanding each with a new parasol. Regina scowled.

Mr. James looked down at her and then over her head. His face broke into a broad smile. "I was wondering when you'd get back from the Continent," he said, extending one of his hands. Regina looked startled, before realizing that he was not addressing her. She turned around to see whom he was addressing.

In front of her were several people, mostly young, and all very well dressed, the women in pretty pastel muslins, the gentlemen in well-cut coats and breeches. "James," one of the older males said, "you've saved me a trip. I was planning to visit you tomorrow."

"A likely story," said Mr. James, laughing. The two men shook hands, and then everyone from the one group blended with the other. Regina found herself staring into the entranced gray eyes of a very nice-looking young man.

The gentleman bowed and swept off his hat, revealing fine blond hair. "Fair lady," he said to her, "you see before you your undying slave."

Regina smiled, determined to put her distressing feelings about the earl out of her mind. Besides, she found the fellow very pleasant—and his attitude toward her did its bit to make her feel better. "I've always wanted an undying slave," she teased.

Again, he bowed. His gray eyes twinkled. "Do you have a name, fair lady? It would make it easier for me to serve you if you did."

"Miss Hammond," she said primly.

"Miss Hammond. Ah, that is beautiful. Indeed, I've never heard a name I liked more."

He was being foolish, but Regina found she enjoyed his manner. If only Lord Audlin were as playful and agreeable.

She swiveled her head to look for him. He was grinning at two young women who gazed at him with adoring glances. Had they no shame? Had *he* none? She was glad that they'd had that dustup and she was quit of him. Who wanted a man whose admirers needed to be beaten off with a stick—let alone a man who seemed to want to beat *her* off with a stick?

The earl glanced up just then and saw her watching him. His eyes went flat and cold.

She would not let him see that he was hurting her. Turning back to the young man, she gave him a ravishing smile.

"Oh, my God," he said, "I'm done for. When can I see you again? Will you let me visit you soon? Is there anything I can get for you? Pearls? Diamonds? My mother and six sisters as handmaidens?"

Regina giggled, drawing Mr. James's attention. "My dear, let me introduce this gentleman to you. He is Mr. Theodore Burnham, a neighbor of ours and the rapscallion son of my friend who stands over there." He jerked his head to the side as he said this, indicating that the man in question was standing nearby.

"How do you do," she said, curtsying.

"A few minutes ago I did poorly. Now I am in alt, and it is all because of you. Shall I get a special license for us? I can leave this minute for London."

Mr. James's laughter joined hers. He is not jealous, Regina realized with some surprise, and that is because he does not care about me anymore. She wondered if he was aware of that. Somehow she did not think so.

She looked at Sally, who, though surrounded by young people, was staring at Mr. James. What was keeping them apart? she wondered. Surely it was not their loyalty to her.

Oh, yes, it was. It had to be—which meant it was her responsibility to do something about the situation. Very well, she thought, unconsciously nodding her head. She would.

She was jarred out of her reverie by Mr. Burnham saying joyously, "You will? I am the luckiest man in the world, then."

Regina's eyebrows went up. Apparently she had just agreed to something Mr. Burnham had asked her, but what it was she had no idea.

He turned to the others. "You'll all come, won't you?"

"Come to what?" Sally asked.

"Why to the ball—a hop, really, I suppose—which we're giving a few evenings hence. I know it's short notice, but so was the decision to have a ball." He grinned. "Indeed, I just decided a minute ago. You won't mind if we don't have white soup, will you?"

Everyone agreed that he would not—in fact, loathed white soup—and would be happy to attend the ball.

Mr. Burnham turned back to Regina. "You will not forget that you have promised to dance a waltz and the supper dance with me, will you?"

So that was what she had agreed to. Why not? The more she stayed out of the earl's arms, the better off she would be. "As though I would," she said.

Still, she waited through the whole next day for the earl to ask her to save those dances for him. To her acute misery, he never said a word about them, or even mentioned the ball.

Mrs. Eckle did, however. "I am sorry, girls," she said, after calling them into her dressing room that evening, "but I've thought about it and thought about it and can come to no other decision. It would not be appropriate for you to attend the Burnhams' ball."

"Mama, why not?" Sally cried. "You don't expect us to disgrace you, do you?" Without waiting for an answer, she said, "We know how to behave, and we know how to dance. You needn't worry about us, need she, Regina?"

Regina, who still hadn't opened her mouth to reply to Mrs. Eckle, merely shook her head. She was thinking, however, that it might not be so dreadful if they did not receive permission to go. If the earl were to refuse to pay her any notice, she'd just as soon stay at home.

"Of course, I wouldn't worry about either one of you—although you have been behaving a bit peculiarly lately, Sally. It is because you girls are not yet out. It would be improper for you to attend a ball."

Regina waited for Sally to launch into a whole mass of arguments. Instead she stuck out her chin and said through tight lips, "You must let us go, Mama."

"Sarah Eckle, don't you dare talk to me in such a demanding tone. What is wrong with you?"

Sally hung her head. "I'm sorry. It's just that I want to go to the ball. I want to go, and I want to dance with Mr. James . . . and, uh, others, of course . . . and I want to go."

Mrs. Eckle looked at her daughter as though the girl had just metamorphosed before her eyes into something strange and unfamiliar. "Oh, very well," she said helplessly, "you may go, but remember, I expect you to behave in a modest fashion and not draw attention to yourselves, either of you."

Nodding only a little skeptically at Sally's promises of perfect behavior, Mrs. Eckle sent them off then.

Once they were back in the bedroom they shared, Sally turned to her friend with a giggle. "We did it. I'm so thrilled. Won't this ball be exciting?"

Regina looked at her sadly. She wasn't excited. How could she be, pining after a man who did not want her, except occasionally when he felt the urge to kiss someone? What a fool she was. At that moment she made a vow to herself that she would ignore the earl the night of the ball. She would dance with Mr. Burnham and anyone else who asked her, and she would enjoy herself. The vow gave her strength.

Thus, when she appeared in the breakfast room the next morning to find the earl seated by himself at the cloth-covered table, she was able to face him with fortitude. "Good morning, my lord," she said calmly.

"Good morning to you. Did you sleep well?"

"Why would I not?" she asked.

"Right." He put a bit of sirloin on his fork, then added some egg and potato, and popped the whole into his mouth. "Would you pour me some coffee, please?"

By now her hand was trembling. The sad truth was that she was not able to keep her composure around Lord Audlin no matter how much she resolved to do so. But he—how could he sit there so calmly eating, as though there was nothing else on his mind but feeding his stomach, the whole while she was coming apart inside? Regina spilled coffee on the tablecloth.

"I'm sorry," she said, feeling very young and gauche.

"It doesn't matter, as long as you didn't pour it on my lap."

He was joking, trying to be pleasant. She gazed up at him, ready to return his smile. He was already looking grave, however.

"I . . . I . . ." she stuttered. Casting about for a topic of conversation, she said, "I am sure we are all eager to attend the Burnhams' ball."

"You are making an assumption, Regina. I am not."

"I suppose when one has attended as many balls as you have, another one means nothing."

He put down his fork. "It depends."

Her brown eyes enormous, she gazed over at him. "On what?"

"You have egg on your face," he said, staring at her intently.

Was he trying to humble her, put her in her place? Regina's chin jutted out. She would not permit it. "Where is it?" she asked.

"On your lip."

"Good. I want it there. I am saving it in case I get hungry later."

The earl began to laugh before leaning over to wipe her lip gently with his napkin. "You're an odd sort of girl," he said, his voice suddenly tender.

"Am I? How am I odd?"

"You are beautiful, but you do not seem to care about that."

"Why do you say that?"

He leaned back in his chair as though considering the subject. "You did not mind getting dirty when we slid down the hill. You did not mind getting wet when you fell in the water—"

"You pulled me in," she said, interrupting him.

"So I did. And you did not mind having egg on your face. Practically any other female I know would have had fits. You're different. Oh, yes, Regina, you are different, inside and out."

"Is that bad?" she asked.

"In general, or for me?"

"For you?" she said in a near whisper.

He rose from his seat and stood behind it. "Very bad."

"And why is that?"

The earl grasped his chair as though it were a shield that could protect him from her. He bit his lip, then said, "You are the sort of girl one marries and cherishes, Regina, not the sort with whom one has a casual flirtation."

What was wrong with that? What was he trying to say? "Yes?"

"Did you know that at one time I considered getting you to stop your pursuit of my uncle"—he raised his hand when she began to object—"to stop your pursuit of my uncle by offering for you myself?"

"But . . . but you never did."

"No, and I won't. Do you know why?"

She looked down at her lap. "It must be because you cannot bear to marry me, not even to save your uncle."

His smile was self-mocking. "Is that what you think? The truth is that I do not wish to marry anyone at present, but especially I do not wish to marry a girl like you."

One tiny tear escaped from Regina's eye and slid down her skin. "Thank you very much," she said.

"Wait, I am not trying to be cruel. You have not heard my reason. It is because I am not ready to commit myself to a woman the way I would have to commit myself to you. You'd drown me in honey, Regina, and I'd be caught fast and never get free. I don't want that."

What was there for Regina to say? She could hardly argue with him.

Lord Audlin made as though to turn to the door but stopped. "I've decided not to go to the ball. I have other plans."

"I wanted to dance with you." Regina's voice was sad. "Just once? No?"

"No," the earl said grimly.

"You won't even give me that. You must really dislike me, my lord, despite your words."

"Dislike you? I don't think so. The point is, I am determined not to love you, Regina. Go to the ball, and dance with Theo Burnham. He seems very taken with you. In fact, I'd wager that if you give him but a little encouragement, he will offer for you. If ever a man was bewitched, it is he."

Regina was a woman scorned. "You mind your own affairs," she said heatedly. "I am well able to take care of mine, and that includes deciding what I want to do about Mr. Burnham, and your uncle, too.''

Without saying another word, the earl left her.

Regina stared at the door through which the earl had disappeared. ''I lied,'' she said. ''I am not able to take care of my affairs at all. If I were, you would love me to distraction.''

~*Chapter 8*

THE NEXT MORNING Regina awoke to the sound of rain hitting the windowpanes. She sighed, although it was not because she disliked rain. In truth, she was one of that probably small number of Englishwomen who actually enjoyed looking at it and walking in it, and didn't even mind getting a bit wet from it.

No, the cause of her sigh was the state of her relations with the earl. He was in a fair way to breaking her heart. Still, she could not seem to stay away from him, or he from her, for that matter—except in the instance of the ball.

And marriage. She believed him when he said he would not marry her. But why wouldn't he? He would have to marry sometime; most men did, if only to get an heir. Then why not her?

He'd told her why, of course, but she did not believe he'd said the whole of it. Perhaps he did not even know the whole of it. Could it be that his very attraction to her made him resent and dislike her? Did he fear that any softer feelings for her might give her a power over him that he could not tolerate? Was he afraid of love?

Sally's sleepy voice interrupted her unhappy musings. "Regina, what are you doing? You have the oddest expression on your face."

"I was thinking about the rain," Regina said, which was at least partially true. "I was wondering if I wanted to get out of bed now and talk a walk in it. If I decide that I do, would you like to join me?"

Sally shuddered. "You really are strange sometimes,

Regina. Walk in the rain, indeed! I am not a duck, and neither are you.''

Regina patted her friend's shoulder. "Go to sleep. As for me, I shall get dressed and go downstairs. I am hungry, and want my breakfast.''

Apparently pleased to be allowed to continue to sleep, Sally gave her friend a drowsy smile and turned over. Regina, meanwhile, arose and began to try to dress herself. Fortunately her maid arrived in time to help her with the tapes she could not reach.

Then, ignoring the maid's look of surprise, Regina took a purple mantle from the wardrobe and tiptoed from the room. She had decided to forgo her breakfast, for a while at any rate. What she wanted more than anything at that moment was to be outdoors and be able to drink in the deliciously cool, damp air. Maybe such a draught would prove to be the panacea for her muzzy thoughts.

By the time she snuck down the backstairs and went out into the weather through a side door, the pounding rain had dwindled to a fine mist. As light as Indian gauze, it spread over her face and spangled her thick, dark brown hair.

Like magic, Regina's heavy mood disappeared. It had been washed away by the spring rain. She drew in a deep breath, then started to walk. Soon she found herself in one of the brick-walled gardens. She spread her mantle upon a wet stone bench, seated herself, and looked about her.

The garden was beautiful, full of newly leaved vines and pale spring flowers. It smelled delightful, too, the sweet scent of flowers combining with the clean odor of damp earth and newly washed growing things. Regina could hear the chirping of several birds. She relaxed and put up her face to the rain. A little smile touched her lips.

It was thus that the earl found her. "Beauty on a purple mantle,'' he said.

"What are you doing here?'' Regina cried, her feeling of serenity instantly leaving her. "Won't you ever leave me alone?'' She jumped to her feet and started to walk to where a gate led to another garden.

"Don't go. I promise not to disturb you,'' the earl said.

But he did disturb her. His mere presence caused her blood to flow faster and her heart to beat harder. "I wanted to be by myself this morning," she said. "Um . . . sometimes I get tired of groups of people."

He reached her and put a hand on her shoulder. "I do not blame you. I do, too. Fortunately two individuals do not constitute a group."

Regina moved her shoulder in an attempt to dislodge his hand. As always, his touch created warm feelings in her that frightened her. The earl removed his hand. "Tell me," he said quietly, looking down at her, "don't you mind the rain? It's dampening your hair and causing it to go all curly."

Regina backed off from him. "I like my hair like that," she said, sounding young and nervous, "and I like the rain. It makes me grow."

The earl burst into laughter. "You are the most unusual girl. Despite your looks, you don't act like a beauty at all. But I've told you that before. In truth, you don't act like anyone else I've ever met. You don't mind dirt and you do like rain, yes, and all sorts of other untidy, elemental things. You're a mystery to me, Regina."

Then that made two of them with the same type of problem. All she said however, was, "Am I? I think I'm ordinary, except, perhaps, in that I suppose I enjoy feeling things."

"Do you, Regina?" The earl's voice had suddenly gone husky. "What else do you like to feel?" His fingers moved across the petal-soft skin of her face. "Do you like to feel me stroking your face?"

In truth, she adored it. If she'd been a cat, the intensity of her pleasure would have made her arch her back and purr. But he must not know that. "No," she said quickly, backing away, "I don't."

The earl's hand dropped. "That is too bad," he said, "for I like it very well. Are you afraid of me, Regina?"

She became all bluster. "I? Afraid of you? That is ridiculous. You're harmless."

The earl's blue eyes narrowed. "Am I? I do not think I am."

Neither did she. Although she did not believe for a minute that he would ever inflict an injury on her, he had already hurt her peace of mind. No other male had ever affected her as he did, certainly not the men who hung about her London town house hoping for a glimpse of her, and certainly not Mr. James. "I know you would not use violent measures with me," she said seriously.

The earl seemed to consider her words. "As you said, I would not do that. There are other ways, however. If I touched your face every day, you would get used to that intimacy and accept it, I believe. Then I might touch your neck and run my hands down your arms from your shoulders to your wrists. Soon, I think, you would come to expect such caresses and even long for them. After that, I might touch you here." He let his fingertips rest against the high swell of her breasts for just an instant before removing his hands from her.

"How dare you!" Regina cried, badly shaken. "You have no right."

"I won't argue with that," he said after a moment. "I do not. Those pleasures are for your husband, not for me. There, that is fair warning of my lack of intentions, is it not?"

"You already gave me fair warning yesterday," she said. "Don't you remember?"

He nodded.

"I do not need any more warnings, my lord. Save them for some other little fool. Besides, I do not wish to marry you. I'd rather have your uncle any day."

The earl's expression grew dark. "It's my uncle again, is it? I'd thought you'd given up on that idea. Let me tell you once more, Miss Hammond, you won't get him, not as long as I have anything to do with it. Keep that in mind, and save yourself a fruitless effort."

"Too kind," she said cuttingly. "Now let me return the favor. Stop threatening me, and save yourself some trouble. As I've already told *you,* I am not easily frightened off."

His Lordship's handsome face was implacable. "We shall see."

Oh, he enraged her. She was in a temper now. She stepped nearer to the edge of a puddle of muddy water and began moving her booted right foot back and forth, touching the edge of the little pool, and then pulling back.

"Don't you dare," the earl said, staring at her foot as though it were a snake and he a mesmerized bird.

Regina's foot moved faster. It kicked at the water. The water splashed on the earl's highly polished Hessians. "Dear me," she said, "how clumsy of me. Perhaps you had better stay far away from me lest another such accident happen. Good-bye, my lord."

She showed him her back and walked off, but turned once before she went through the gate. The earl was still standing near the puddle, hands clenched, looking down at his boots as the dirty water marked a path on their previously unblemished surfaces.

Regina returned to the house and made her way back to her room. Sally was no longer in it, for which Regina felt thankful. She needed a respite before facing the others. She dried her hair, then changed her gown for a shiny blue-and-pink chintz day dress and replaced her boots with slippers. After that she went to the breakfast room.

Sally was there. "I suppose you went for a walk after all, didn't you?" she said somewhat petulantly. "Your face is all pink. If you catch a cold, don't blame me."

"I won't," Regina replied before heaping her plate with ham, eggs, and mushrooms; she felt very hungry.

"Look, it's begun raining harder again," Sally said accusingly, as though the condition of the weather were Regina's failed responsibility. "What are we going to do with ourselves today?"

The only thing Regina was certain she wanted to do was stay away from the earl. "I don't know," she said, shaking her head.

Sally buttered a roll with minimal enthusiasm. "I suppose we'll have to keep to the indoors the entire day. Do you think the earl and Mr. James will spend much time with us?

If they would, I would not care about being confined to the house for a week.''

Regina shrugged. ''Your mama once told me that gentlemen in the country usually go about their own pursuits and leave the ladies to theirs. Didn't you ever hear her say that?''

''And leave the ladies to theirs? That's horrible.''

Regina smiled. ''You only think so because you want to be with the earl.''

Sally took a bite out of the roll, then set it carefully upon a small plate. ''I do,'' she said, ''but I like being with Mr. James, too, Regina, because he's restful. When I am with him, on excursions, at meals, and in the evenings, I always feel that everything will be all right. When I am with the earl, I always feel it probably won't—at least not for me.''

Nor for me, either, Regina thought. Determined not to sink into the doldrums, she chatted about this and that for a few minutes before saying, ''I like your gown. The red and blue ribbons are so very pretty and cheerful. You should even be able to cheer the earl.''

Sally cocked her head and looked at her friend. ''What do you mean? Do you think he is uncheerful?''

Regina had no intention of telling Sally, or anyone else, what she had done to the earl. ''No, but he cannot be altogether happy as long as he continues to believe I mean to ensnare his uncle for my own evil ends.''

Sally smoothed down her day dress with absentminded fingers. ''Regina, are you certain that you've told him clearly how you feel?''

Instead of replying to the question, Regina said, ''I've had enough to eat. Have you? If you have, let us go and find the others, if they are awake yet.''

Of course, she knew that the earl was awake, but she could not tell Sally that without telling her how she knew it. ''I'd wager the earl is already up,'' she said.

''And likely Mr. James,'' Sally added. ''You forgot Mr. James.''

Regina paused before the door leading into the hall and

turned about. "You, however, never do," she said, her tone speculative. "Are you sure it is the earl you dote upon?"

"I cannot answer that. I am too confused."

Regina was beginning not to believe her. Now, if only Sally would fall head over ears in love with Mr. James and he would fall in love with Sally, that would be splendid.

It might be splendid, but it seemed impossible given Mr. James's apparent determination to wed Regina and add her to his collection of beautiful objects. Why didn't men know what was best for them, she thought with annoyance. And added, And why do I not know for myself?

The question was struck from her mind by the appearance of Lady Sanding with Regina's papa. They both looked very happy; however, when Mr. Hammond saw Regina, his face took on a guilty expression. What was there for him to feel guilty about? she wondered. Surely they couldn't have been kissing or . . . She stared at her papa as though she'd never seen him before, which, in a sense, was the truth. This romantic gentleman was a stranger to her.

He's leaving me, she thought painfully. What shall I do? She had no answer, so she murmured an unintelligible excuse for going from the room and walked away.

Unfortunately she was followed by Lady Sanding, who had apparently left Mr. Hammond behind to rush after his daughter. "I was wanting to talk with you," Lady Sanding said heartily. "We need to get to know each other better."

Regina looked at her coolly. "Why is that, my lady?"

"Why not?" Lady Sanding replied, laughing.

Regina could have given her several reasons, but they would all have come to the same thing: she did not want her papa to love another woman. She was jealous!

"How shameful," she muttered, embarrassed by her unworthy reaction.

"What is that you said, Miss Hammond?"

Regina might think her feelings shameful, and she might be embarrassed, but she still felt jealous. *Know thyself* might be good advice, but then what was one to do with the information?

"Nothing," she replied. "Please excuse me, Lady Sanding. There is something I must do in my room now." She hesitated, then put out her hand to the other woman. "Perhaps we can talk later."

Upstairs in her bedroom, Regina wondered why she had extended her hand, however reluctantly, to Lady Sanding. She thought about it quite a bit until, finally, she came to a conclusion she had to accept: she could hardly fault anyone for feeling an attraction to another person, for, in spite of herself, she felt such an attraction to the eminently unwilling and unsuitable Earl of Audlin.

Her moments of honesty came to an end a short time later upon the crashing open of the bedroom door. "You must join me downstairs," Sally told her. "The men have gone off, and it's ever so boring here."

"If you like," Regina said, making a conscious effort to recall her good nature. "I'll come downstairs and be bored as well."

The rest of the rainy day was spent in playing cards and doing handwork. These activities seemed to please Mrs. Eckle and Lady Sanding well enough. For Regina and Sally, however, the hours dragged by.

Indeed, it was not until after a long and tedious dinner, from which the men absented themselves, that the day began to alter for the better. The ladies were gathered in the blue drawing room, their usual meeting place after the evening meal, making desultory conversation. "I think you look lovely in white, Miss Hammond," Lady Sanding told her. "It is so dramatic with your dark hair and eyes."

"Thank you, Your Ladyship."

"You, on the other hand, Miss Eckle, should never wear white."

Since Sally was woolgathering, and thus not paying any heed to Lady Sanding's remarks, no harm was done in that direction. Mrs. Eckle, however, bristled quite noticeably. Regina was just about to thrust herself into the conversation, to avert a possible quarrel, when the gentlemen providentially walked in.

It was amazing how animated the ladies suddenly became. Even Regina, who was not pleased with her papa, and quite displeased with the earl, brightened considerably.

Mr. James seated himself on the sofa between Regina and Sally. "What have you ladies been doing today? I hope you found plenty with which to amuse yourselves."

"We've been talking and having the best time," Lady Sanding replied, ignoring the other females' incredulous looks. "However, we are pleased to see you."

"Yes," Sally agreed enthusiastically. "Perhaps now we can have some fun."

The earl grinned at her. "How will we manage to do that, Miss Eckle?"

"I don't know. Oh, yes, I do; we can play games," Sally said. "You play games, don't you?"

"Some people believe I do," the earl replied. "What sort of game would you like to play?"

Apparently Sally's forte was general ideas, not specific suggestions. "I do not know," she said.

He turned to Regina. "What sort of game would you like to play, Miss Hammond? I'm sure you are an expert."

"I could hardly be more expert than you," she said with a wide, patently insincere smile.

"We could play Crambo," Mr. James offered hastily.

"Crambo? Yes, let's," Sally agreed, bestowing an approving look upon him. "You go first, please, Mr. James. I'm sure you know ever so many poems."

He rose and glanced about. "We'll have to form a circle. Audlin, how about helping with these chairs."

Soon they were all seated upon an assortment of Adam and Sheraton chairs, the earl between Sally and Regina. "Well, Uncle?" he asked.

"Let me see." Mr. James leaned forward, his elbows on his knees, his head propped between his hands. "I have it," he said, straightening. "Sir Philip Sidney: 'My true love hath my heart, and I have his.'"

"That is too easy," said Lady Sanding, who sat to the right of him. "Thousands of words must rhyme with *his*."

Mr. James grinned, obviously enjoying himself. "Then

you will have no difficulty making up a rhyming sentence. I am happy for you.''

"Wait," she said. "Biz, ciz, diz. How dreadful; nothing rhymes with *his*. Fiz. Giz." Her Ladyship grimaced. "I give up, you awful man."

"You give up very quickly," Mr. James said with a laugh.

Lady Sanding looked at Mr. Hammond. "Only when I do not care about the issue."

Mr. James raised his brows slightly, then smiled and said, "Now it is your turn to provide a rhyming sentence, Lady Sanding."

"Me? Oh, no. I do not know any poems."

"By Jove," said Mr. Hammond, "neither do I, at least none I could say in front of a lady."

Soon everyone else had disclaimed knowing any suitable poems and bowed out, except for the earl and Regina. "You go first," she said.

The earl thought a minute, then said, "Andrew Marvell: 'Had we but world enough and time, this coyness, Lady, were no crime.' "

Regina blushed, convinced that the earl had chosen the line as a message to her. Her "coyness" a crime, indeed! But what could she reply? She could not think, let alone find a rhyme.

"As the poem suggests, time is running out," he said, grinning.

Regina lowered her eyes. "Had we but world enough and time, this coyness still would be no crime."

A direct hit! Regina laughed.

"That isn't fair," the Earl protested. He, too, was laughing, although the expression in his eyes suggested that he was not entirely amused. "You cannot use the same words to rhyme."

"Of course, she can," said Mr. James. "You were fairly beaten, Audlin. Now, give us another or leave the field to Miss Hammond."

The earl gazed into Regina's wide, dark eyes. "I'll never

do that. Michael Drayton: 'Since there's no help, come let us kiss and part.' "

Regina flushed and her eyes became wider and darker. "I'd far rather part than give you my heart. My lord?" she shot back.

Sally rose hastily to her feet, drawing attention away from the combatants and to herself. "Why don't we play something else?" she asked brightly. "Something without any words."

Mr. Hammond looked puzzled. "Without any . . . What do you mean?" He gasped as Lady Sanding pushed her elbow against his side. "Right," he said. "Without any words. What do you suggest, Sally?"

"We could play blindman's buff."

A picture of the blindfolded earl running his hands over her face and body in order to identify her flashed into Regina's mind, bringing with it a burst of heat that spread all over her skin. "I do not want to," she said.

"Nor would I let you girls," Mrs. Eckle said. "Sarah, think again."

Sally pursed her lips, but then said obediently. "Yes, Mama. Um . . . we could play hide and go seek."

"You are not in short coats, Sarah," Mrs. Eckle scolded.

"No, but I am tired of sitting still, Mama. I believe that is all I've done today."

"Hide and go seek sounds like fun," the earl said. "I do not see why we could not play that game. Mrs. Eckle, will you change your mind?"

"I defer to you, my lord. However, I think we need to put limits on the game. We cannot have ourselves racing all over this vast house."

"Such fun," said Lady Sanding, sounding as enthusiastic as Sally. "Let us confine it to this room and the rooms on either side of it. Will that be all right?" Everyone nodded. "And let the seekers have a limit of half an hour to find us."

"Let us have but one seeker and one hider at a time," Mr. James suggested. "Otherwise it will be pandemonium here. Now, whom shall we enlist as the seeker?"

Everyone laughingly refused the privilege.

"I see that I must sacrifice myself for the good of the group," said the earl. "So be it."

Regina raised her eyes to him. "I do not expect that you will be very expert at being the seeker, my lord," she said, "not having had much practice."

Mr. Hammond frowned at his daughter. "Half the time when I listen to you I think you are talking in some sort of code, Regina. What did you mean by that remark to Lord Audlin?"

"She was just saying nonsense, to be amusing," said the earl, before Regina could reply to her papa. "Pay it no heed. I certainly won't. Tell me, Miss Hammond, would you be willing to be the hider I am seeking? Then we can prove whether or not I am as poor a seeker as you think."

Before Regina could reply, Sally said, "Let me be the hider. I am the one who most needs the exercise."

The earl agreed readily, to Regina's disappointment. Why had he asked her if he was so willing to accept another in her place? She hoped he would be unable to find Sally and have to concede defeat.

The earl, apparently, was not concerned about his possible inabilities and, with an easy grin, covered his eyes. Sally crept off to crouch behind a large, brocade-covered armchair in a corner of the drawing room. Everyone else looked on, laughing and making silly suggestions.

"Ready!" Sally called.

It was not long before the earl located her, probably because he bent over to look beneath the chair and thus saw her. Then it was Sally's turn. "Whom shall you choose to be the hider?" her mama asked.

Sally looked first at the earl and then at Mr. James. "I choose Mr. James," she said after a moment. "Ah . . . that is only because the earl has already played." She looked appealingly at Mr. James. "Please go and hide, sir, and let me attempt to find you."

While she covered her eyes Mr. James looked about the room. Then he snuck behind one of the beautiful turquoise silk curtains that covered the windows. A second later he popped his head out, put a finger to his lips to silence the noisy group, and called, "Ready!"

Sally insisted upon starting her exploration with the room to the left of the drawing room. Then she examined the right. Finally, back in the drawing room she glanced at the windows. There, where they had been in clear view the whole time, she saw Mr. James's evening slippers sticking out from behind the material. "I've found you," she cried, flinging herself at the curtain. It went down, Mr. James went down, and Sally went down in a mix of rods, silk material, and arms and legs.

"I do not know what I am going to do with that girl," said Mrs. Eckle, red-faced. "Sally, you are the worst hoyden I've ever seen."

Mr. James, although still seated on the floor, emerged from behind a thick swag of turquoise. "Don't scold her," he said. "She is full of life and makes everything wonderful."

Finally it was the earl's turn again. "I pick Miss Hammond to be the hider," he said. "Miss Hammond, are you willing?"

She wanted to say that she wasn't, but with everyone looking at her so expectantly, she knew she could not disappoint the group. "If you wish," she said in a low voice. "But you must give me time to hide."

"As much as you like—although it may not do you any good," he added in a low, languorous voice.

It is just a game, Regina kept telling herself. It isn't important. But it was, and she knew it. More than anything, she wanted to bring the earl to defeat and hear him admit it. Now where could she hide so that he'd not find her in a whole half hour of trying?

In the room to the left, while she'd been trailing Sally, she'd noticed a section of the wall that had trim around it as though it contained a closet. If it did, that might be a perfect place, especially because no one else had chosen it. On tiptoe, she snuck from the drawing room, went into the adjoining room, and poked and pried at the likely spot. Nothing moved.

"Are you ready?" the earl called.

Regina gave one last desperate poke—and the wall opened. There was, indeed, a space inside, and behind it a narrow staircase going up to the next floor. "Ready," she cried, then pulled the door to behind her.

My, it was hot inside the wall, and dusty. She hoped she didn't sneeze and give herself away.

After what seemed like an hour, at least, when nothing happened, Regina wished she hadn't picked her hiding place. Not only was it cramped and uncomfortable, but also she feared that the earl and the other guests would get tired of looking for her and drift off. Besides, she was thirsty and getting thirstier.

She had just about decided to give herself up when she heard voices and then banging sounds against the outer wall. Let the earl find her; by this time she could only be grateful.

"Are you sure there is a door here?" she heard the earl say. "If there is, I cannot open it."

"I'm inside," Regina called. "I'll open it."

Alas, as much as she twisted and turned, banged and pushed, she could not get the panel open. "You must try again," she said. "I cannot find the mechanism to open this after all."

There was more banging, something that sounded like a curse, and an offer made to have the wall torn out. Then there was quiet. She hoped that whatever the others meant to do, they would do it in haste.

Detecting a sound behind her, she turned around in the narrow space—and heard her gown rip as she did. "I'm down here," she called up the stairs in a wavering voice.

There was a dim light above the stairs, then the sound of someone coming down. Regina lifted her head to see who her rescuer was. She expected it to be one of the estate workmen. Instead, it was the earl, and he did not look best pleased.

"Thank you for finding me, my lord," she said. "You have a cobweb on your head."

"Oh, good," he said. He gave her face a pat. "Now, Regina, move out of the way if you can. My uncle would like to get this door open.'' As she attempted to squeeze to one side the earl thrust out his hand and hit the door behind her. It opened, causing Regina nearly to fall outside.

She straightened. There stood all the others. They were clapping and cheering. As for the earl, he put his head close to hers, the cobweb still crazily hanging on to his dark hair. ''I told you I'd find you,'' he said in a low voice.

She smiled. ''So you did.''

''But what the devil am I going to do with you, Regina? That is always the unresolved question, isn't it?''

~Chapter 9

IT WAS THE night of the Burnhams' ball. Eager to dance and spend the evening with Mr. James, Sally dressed with special care. She wore a white muslin gown with a demitrain, the gown brightened by a reembroidered green silk sash of Regina's and a green ruff she'd purchased in Tunbridge Wells, white silk stockings, and white slippers that tied about her ankles.

Knowing she would not be dancing with the earl, Regina did not concern herself about dressing with special care. Indifferently she put on a filmy white gown trimmed with silver ribbon knots chosen by the maid when Regina refused to make a selection. She wore it over a silver slip and, like Sally, had on white silk stockings and white slippers with ties. In her heavy, curly hair, she wore lengths of silver ribbon plaited with a rope of pearls belonging to Mrs. Eckle. Although she had not tried, Regina looked exquisite.

Not that it mattered to her, even after everyone in their party had complimented her, Mr. James going so far as to say she reminded him of Botticelli's Venus or Michelangelo's Madonna, he wasn't sure which. To Regina's mind, there was no reason for her to give a thought to how she looked. Indeed, she felt that there was no reason for her to go to the Burnhams' at all. It was unfortunate that her papa would not hear of her being absent.

When they arrived at the Burnhams' Palladian-style mansion, the two girls went up to the ballroom floor ahead of the others. "Isn't it beautiful?" Sally asked, peeking into

133

the ballroom. "Have you ever seen a more beautiful setting?"

Regina had to agree that she had not. Of course, since neither of them had ever attended a ball before, it was not strange that they should be impressed with the candlelit chandeliers reflected in tall pier glasses between floor-to-ceiling windows, the polished parquet floor, and delicate chairs with Sardinian-blue cushions that were set around the periphery of the pale green room. Everything gleamed and shone and sparkled, as did the guests, many of whom were young and quite pleasant to look at.

Because the girls were waiting for the others in their group to doff their wraps and come up the stairs, they could only peek inside the ballroom as yet but not enter it. "Why don't they hurry?" Sally whined, twitching with excitement. "The evening will be over before we have even danced one dance." She took a deep breath. "You won't mind if Mr. James asks me to dance, will you?"

Perhaps this was Regina's chance to let Sally know she was aware of her friend's feeling for Mr. James. "Why do you want to dance with him? I thought it was the earl you cared for."

"The earl isn't here," Sally said quickly.

Regina nodded sadly.

"Would you mind if Mr. James asks me to waltz with him?" her friend went on.

Regina put her hand on Sally's arm. "I don't mind if you dance every waltz with him, Sally. Truly I don't."

"Is that because you are interested in Mr. Burnham now?"

Regina's eyebrows went up in surprise, but then she nodded. Mr. Burnham was as good an excuse as any.

Sally beamed. "Even if my mama says I can't waltz because I'm too young, I will."

"Are you sure you can?" Regina said. "We haven't been taught to waltz yet."

"I won't have to be taught. I'll know how. And if I don't, Mr. James will teach me," her friend said with conviction.

How nice it must be to have so much faith in one's

partner, Regina thought with a sigh. She envied Sally her certitude.

"Would you mind if Mr. James asked me for the supper dance?" Sally now wanted to know. "I would so like to dance the supper dance with him . . . uh . . . since the earl isn't here."

"You might dance everything and anything with him if it were up to me," Regina said. "You needn't ask me about another thing, Sally, truly."

Apparently unable to stop fretting, even after receiving carte blanche from Regina, Sally said, "I suppose it wouldn't be the thing for him to ask me more than twice, would it?" Since she knew as well as Regina that such an action would be highly improper, and cause everyone to gossip, Regina felt she need do no more than shake her head.

Suddenly Sally's piquant face brightened. "Here comes Mr. James—I mean, here comes everyone. Thank the Lord."

Regina gave the rest of their party a half smile, except for her papa and a ravishing-looking Lady Sanding, the latter dressed in black and white, it went without saying, and aglitter from head to toe with diamonds. In Regina's opinion, they stood much too close to each other and thus deserved the frown she bestowed upon them. People their ages should be discreet, she thought, tugging ferociously at one of her white gloves. Better yet, there should be no reason for them to need to be discreet.

Sally was a different matter. Although lit up like a fireworks display due to Mr. James's presence, joy and excitement blazing out of every pore, she was young and could not help herself. "Let us go in," Miss Eckle said, giving Mr. James a brilliant smile and her mama a little push. "I am certain we must have missed four or five sets already." With a look of despair at her rag-mannered daughter, Mrs. Eckle complied.

They were barely inside the ballroom when Mr. Theodore Burnham left the receiving line and came rushing over to them. He must have been watching for them, Regina thought, since he had not wasted a minute. "I was wondering if I had imagined how beautiful you are," he said, after giving her a deep, exaggerated bow, "but I see that I had not imagined your beauty at all. Indeed, you are more wonderful looking than I recollected."

Although she knew that the gentleman's excessive language was in jest, Regina was embarrassed. Unable to think of what to reply, she gave Mr. Burnham a vapid smile.

"You will dance the first dance and the supper dance with me, will you not?" the ebullient Mr. Burnham went on. "Do not say no. If you do, I shall have to take to drink, gamble away my properties, and end up in the Fleet. You couldn't be so unkind as to let me destroy myself over love for you, could you?"

"No, not that unkind," Regina said, frankly laughing now. Even though he was being silly, his words helped a bit to heal the hurt inflicted by the earl's attitude, not to mention his absence.

Once their group was through the receiving line, Mr. Burnham did his best to keep the other young men away from Regina. However, he was not noticeably successful.

"Who is this fair charmer?" a duke bustled over to ask. He had to stand directly next to Mr. Burnham to hear the latter's mumbled reply. After that and introductions all around, he put his name down for a waltz.

"Lovely lady, will you dance with me?" another gentleman asked with a smile and a wink.

Soon her card was filled. I will have a good time tonight, she told herself. I will if I die in the attempt.

Would the earl grieve even a little if he were to hear of her untimely death? she wondered. She pictured herself white and still upon a bier, the earl gazing down at her. Little birds came and dropped brown seeds and red berries into her garments. Regina was so touched by the picture she'd created, she almost cried. Providentially Mrs. Eckle gave her a talk, which mostly dealt with not getting carried away by one's successes at a provincial ball, and Regina regained her customary good sense.

The first dance was a minuet, old-fashioned, of course,

but insisted upon by the elder Mr. Burnham. After that came a series of country dances. Regina danced every one and promenaded with her partner after each.

She had just finished promenading with a tall, skinny youth upon their completing the "Dressed Ship," a country dance for as many as would. The next dance was to be a waltz. "I am here, fair lady," Theo Burnham said enthusiastically. "I claim you as my own."

"But you can't," she said. "I've promised this dance to someone else. Here he comes now."

They both turned to look at the smiling young man moving toward her. Regina hoped Mr. Burnham wasn't going to be difficult with her new partner; he seemed to have forgotten that his avowals of love were only in jest. She started to say something to him but forgot what it was when a large hand came down lightly on her shoulder. She whirled around—and thought for a second or two that she might faint. The owner of the proprietary hand was not any of the gentlemen to whom she'd promised dances but the handsome, elusive, glorious, and heartless Earl of Audlin. He smelled of cologne and spirits, and there was a reckless air about him.

"What are you doing here?" she asked, sounding piqued.

The earl shrugged his black-clad shoulders. "Perhaps I could not stay away."

Regina's face brightened. "Really? Why is that?"

"Do you want me to say it is because of you, minx?"

The brightness disappeared. "Why would I think so?"

The earl's expression grew serious. "Yes, why would you?"

"It doesn't matter what she believes," Mr. Burnham said. "She is dancing next with me."

"Claim someone else, Burnham," the earl responded in a flat tone that somehow managed to seem threatening. "The lady is taken."

"My lord," Theo said, "remove your hand from Miss Hammond and yourself from her presence, or I shall have to run you through."

While the approaching young man, who apparently heard this interchange, veered off, Regina felt the earl's hand tense. It would seem that he took the threat seriously. "You won't run him through," she said, positioning herself in front of the earl.

Theo Burnham blinked, then said in a disillusioned voice, "Oh, it's that way, is it?"

"I don't know what you mean," Regina said, moving closer to Mr. Burnham and away from the earl. She was terribly ashamed about what she had done, although she knew she would do it again if she had to. That was because she could not bear to think of anyone attempting to harm Lord Audlin—except herself.

"Are you having a good time?" Theo's papa asked as he joined them. None of the three answered him. He stared at the young men, both of whom looked decidedly pugnacious. "Are you gamecocks fighting over which of you shall waltz with this young lady? I cannot say I blame you," he said with a laugh. "I'd do it myself if I were younger and less married."

"I'm sorry," Regina said, blushing. "There's been some confusion here, I think. It's . . . uh . . . my fault, I don't doubt."

Mr. Burnham smiled approvingly at her. "You are a nice young woman as well as a beautiful one," he said. "Tell me, is this the first waltz?"

Regina nodded. "I believe so."

"Then I have a solution. You must dance it with the earl, because rank has its privileges, but you must promise the next waltz to my son. Well, what do you think? Am I as wise as Solomon?"

"You are," she said, unwilling to disappoint him by mentioning that she had promised the next waltz to a very eager duke. What was she to do with him?

Mr. Burnham's son had no such compunctions. "What about the supper dance?" he asked belligerently, looking at the earl. "I hope you have no expectation of dancing that with Miss Hammond."

"Of course I have."

"Well, you cannot. There is only one of those, and it is

promised to me." He took hold of Regina's card. "See, there is my name."

The earl rubbed forcefully with a long finger until it disappeared. "Not anymore," he said.

"Just a minute," Regina protested, feeling like an item of merchandise rather than a girl at her first ball. She reddened when the three males glared at her, their response proclaiming that in their opinion, she had no right to interfere; her option was to wait until they decided her fate and then accept it. "I . . . that is, Mr. Burnham signed my card, even if his name has disappeared. Therefore it is he with whom I must dance the supper dance."

"Must?" repeated Theo Burnham, sounding angry as well as disappointed in her response.

"Mr. Burnham?" repeated the earl, merely sounding angry. "Have you no loyalty to a fellow houseguest, Miss Hammond?"

She wanted to ask him why she should. What was it he'd offered her except kisses that tormented and befuddled her and an occasional feeling of fun, camaraderie, and approval? "Loyalty has nothing to do with it," she said primly, then added, "If you wish to waltz with me, you should do so now because the music has started."

"Very well," said the earl, looking at Theo Burnham's face, which had turned a startling shade of red. Regina did not know what to expect.

"It is fortunate for you that you are our guest," Mr. Burnham addressed the earl in a strangled voice. Then, to her relief, he walked away. She felt further relieved when his papa followed him soon after.

Looking up at the victorious earl, she said, "It does not please me that you take my acquiescence for granted, my lord."

He smiled grimly. "You are wrong. With you, my dear, I take nothing for granted."

"I might as well tell you that I do not know how to waltz," she said as though that information would rob him of his desire to dance with her. "You have won very little for your efforts."

This time his smile was sweet. "Let me be the judge of that." He put a finger over her lips before she could reply and murmured into her ear, "As you said, the waltz has begun. Now I am going to take you securely into my arms, Regina, and you are going to follow where I lead. Aren't you, love?"

His speech was so intimate and seductive that it made her want to fling herself at him. It also made her want to run away. "I may not be able to follow you," she said. "Perhaps we should sit down until this dance is over."

One of his dark eyebrows went up and he grinned at her, causing her heart to lurch. "After all I've done to get you? Besides, that is not necessary. I will teach you, Regina. In truth, I want to teach you. I would be disappointed if someone else were to do so first."

Why was he being so serious about a waltz? Before Regina could ask him, the earl stretched out his left hand for her to rest her right hand on. Though they both wore gloves, she was certain she could feel his skin; it burned into hers, hot and hard.

"Now," he said, sounding untouched by passion or anything else, "put your left hand on my right shoulder. Don't be shy."

"I'm not," she said indignantly, but she wasn't telling the truth. Except for those few times he'd kissed her, she had never been so close to him before.

Her breathing quickened. It made her feel light-headed. She had to gain command of herself.

That was no easy task, because the next thing the earl did was put his right arm around her so that his hand was on her back. "Oh," she said with a gasp and tried to pull away, but he would not let her go.

"You smell like heliotrope on top," he said, sniffing her hair. He bent his head so that his lips almost touched her neck. "And roses everywhere else."

Blushing, Regina bent her head. "Mrs. Eckle let us borrow her Pears soap," she babbled. "It is scented with otto of roses."

"And the heliotrope?"

"I . . . I added that to the rinse water for my hair."

Should she have told him those things? She felt young and naive, but he had asked; besides, she could not seem to control her words. Her knees seemed to have passed out of her control as well.

The earl smiled at her. "Wonderful," he said, referring, she supposed, to the rinse water. "Can you feel the music, Regina? Waltzes are quite different from country dances."

She had been attending only to him, but she would not admit it. "I think so. The measures contain three beats, do they not?"

"How clever you are. That is exactly right. And I am clever, too."

"How so?" she asked, raising her head to gaze deeply into his blue eyes.

"Because I taught you so easily and well. Rotate, rotate," he said as she started to protest his partial usurpation of the credit.

So rotate she did. It did not matter that he teased her. It felt grand to be in the earl's strong arms, twirling about the floor. She could dance this way forever.

"Now," said the earl, "it is time to concentrate solely on me, Regina, as though we were the only two people in this room."

In truth, she felt as though they were alone, and she liked what she felt. It was pure magic to pretend that they were by themselves in the huge room, she in gauzy white and silver and he in elegant black, being carried along in the golden glow of the candlelight by a lilting stream of music.

"Close your eyes for a minute," he said. "Don't be afraid. I won't let anything happen to you. Trust me. This time really trust me and follow the steps with me."

Trust him? Well, she would try. First, however, she looked up at him. "Are . . . are you trying to cast a spell over me, my lord? If you are, I believe you will be successful."

"I wish that were so," he said, his voice husky. He passed a hand over her eyes. Regina obediently closed them. "Good. Not one of the hordes of men who look at you with hungry glances and want to possess you is here anymore. I have you all to myself.''

Regina's eyes flew open and she stumbled.

The earl laughed. ''Do you love me, Regina?''

Taken by surprise, she almost told him the truth, but she stopped herself. How could she tell him she loved him when he'd never given her any indication that he cared for her? Sally might rush headlong into things, but she did not. That wasn't her nature.

''I . . . I like you—sometimes,'' she said.

''Really? I suppose I will have to be satisfied with that, won't I—at least for now?''

His voice and smile were pleasant, but she could tell the spell was broken. Indeed, the whole time it took for the orchestra to finish the waltz, he did not say another word to her.

The music stopped; the waltz was over—and there was Theodore Burnham, his gray eyes sullen, his jaw set in a contentious line, determined to guard her until it was time for him to dance with her again.

Regina began to wonder if he was pretending to be enamored of her or really was. Her intuition suggested a third possibility: that he was enamored of besting the Earl of Audlin. What did it matter? She couldn't bear any of it.

Leaving the two men behind, she fled into the garden. There she remained hidden, until she overheard someone say that it was time to go in to supper.

''I've been looking everywhere for you,'' Theo said upon her reappearance into the ballroom. ''Where have you been?''

''I was outside. It was . . . it was too warm for me in here.''

He smiled. ''For a minute I thought it was going to be too warm for me,'' he said with obvious reference to the earl. She returned his smile, glad that he no longer seemed irate. ''You needn't worry, Miss Hammond. I do not mean to misbehave,'' he said, confirming her supposition. ''Nor do I think the earl does, although I cannot vouch for him.''

Regina shivered.

"You stayed outdoors too long," Mr. Burnham scolded. "Would you like me to fetch a shawl for you?"

How could she tell him that her chill was inside herself, because she could not vouch for the earl either? "It's nothing," she said. "Indeed, I am warmer now."

"Then come." He smiled tenderly, the way she might at one of the wild birds she attracted. "Let me get you something to eat."

Suppressing a grin over the aptness of her comparison, she accepted his arm and walked into an adjoining room with him. It contained a number of round, cloth-covered tables set with bright pink and yellow flowers and several long tables filled with delicious-smelling food and drink. Mr. Burnham escorted her to one of the round tables. "This shall be ours," he said, looking about fiercely at various passing gentlemen despite his promise not to misbehave.

As he went to fill plates for them Regina looked about herself. She was searching for the earl. However, he found her before she did him, as did Lady Sanding, who was on his arm. "May I?" he said, and seated himself next to her, Her Ladyship on his other side.

Regina stared at the beautiful Lady Sanding. She had been certain that Her Ladyship would be the partner of Regina's papa. "Where is my papa?" she asked. Looking discontented, Lady Sanding shook her blond head.

Another unhappy female. That made two of them. Regina wished she could not smell the earl's cologne or feel his body heat. They produced a wave of longing in her. She wished she could fall into his lap.

Mr. Burnham returned just then, balancing two filled plates. When he saw the earl, he nearly dropped them. "Careful," Regina murmured.

Mr. Burnham smiled politely at the others, although Regina could not detect any of his usual good nature. She found herself wishing she had stayed at Fairways that evening.

Her opinion did not change when she beheld her papa enter the room with a woman she did not know. He, too,

commandeered seats at their table, his next to that of Lady
Sanding, to whom he gave a sheepish look.

Regina could not imagine what was going forward. No
one was with anyone with whom she would have expected
that person to be. She would wager without fear of losing
that theirs must be one of the unhappiest tables in the supper
room. All that was lacking were Sally and Mr. James with
partners other than each other.

As though thinking about them had propelled them
forward, they appeared in the entrance to the room. Regina
might have laughed if she hadn't felt so dreadful—Sally
was with the tall, skinny fellow with whom Regina had
danced the "Dressed Ship," and Mr. James was with Mrs.
Eckle. The arrangement made her think of some peculiar
punishments Mr. James had told her about involving someone named Tantalus and someone else named Sisyphus,
both of whom had displeased the gods and were, therefore,
doomed to continuing frustration. At least, she thought with
a sigh, her frustrations and those of her fellows would only
last a few more hours. She hoped she could bear the wait.

She greeted the two newcomers, then looked at her papa.
A single glance told her that there might be trouble in that
quarter. Her papa was drinking a great deal—obviously had
been drinking for some time—and, she feared, getting
drunk. If he were to reach that miserable state, she did not
know what he might do or say.

Putting down his glass, Mr. Hammond stared at Lady
Sanding. "I searched for you," he said, "but I could not
find you."

Her Ladyship sniffed. "You must not have searched very
hard. I have been in the ballroom all evening."

"That is the answer," he said. "I was searching for you
in the card room. That is where I found this lady."

"Mrs. Roundtree, widow," she supplied, since he appeared to have forgotten her name. "We were playing
cards," she went on as if she'd been called up on to do so.
"Mr. Hammond lost."

"He needs me," Lady Sanding said in a whisper to

Regina, ignoring the earl by leaning in front of him as she did.

Regina followed her example. "I am beginning to believe that you may be right."

"We should talk," Her Ladyship added.

Regina nodded. "Perhaps we will."

"How kind of you to wait," the earl said sarcastically, obviously miffed at being nothing more than a backdrop for the two.

"I don't like your tone, Audlin," the younger Mr. Burnham snapped. "You should never speak thus when addressing the divine Miss Hammond. She deserves soft voices, fine food and wine, and the company of the most refined courtiers, such as myself."

The earl laughed. "For your information, she is neither divine nor a princess, Burnham. She is a real, live, exciting woman, and what she *deserves* are hills of dirt to roll down and fishing streams into which to fall."

"I don't know what you are talking about," Theo Burnham said haughtily.

As Regina put her hand to her cheek in worry and Lady Sanding gave Mr. Burnham a warning glance, the earl said coldly, "I didn't think that you would."

"You told me you did not mean to misbehave," Regina said quickly to Mr. Burnham before he could respond. "Please keep your word."

That gentleman, though remaining seated, sketched a bow. "For you, dear Miss Hammond, I would do anything—even tolerate that boorish fellow you seem to have some affection for."

"It's loyalty," she said, grasping at something that had been mentioned before. "We are in the same house party, you know."

"Do you expect me to thank you for that explanation?" the earl addressed her.

Mr. Burnham rose to his feet. "Now, see here, Audlin. . . ."

It was at that point that Sally leaned over and whispered to Regina, "Are you having a good time?"

Regina could not help herself: she began to laugh hysterically.

"Oh, dear," Sally said. "Mama, do something. Regina is . . . she is . . . she isn't herself."

"I will take her out to the garden," said the earl, jumping up.

Mr. Burnham rose as well. "The devil you will. I shall take her to the garden if anyone is to do so. It *is* my garden, or will be when my papa—well, never mind about that."

"I don't want to go to the garden," Regina said. "I've already been there, for ages."

Mr. Burnham's eyes narrowed. "Yes, I did not understand about that at all."

"Leave her alone, Burnham," the earl said harshly, "or I'll make you do so."

Sally looked horrified. "This is the worst ball I've ever been to," she said.

"But, dear," her mama replied, "this is the only ball you've ever been to."

"Yes, and if the rest of them are to be like this, I don't wish to accept invitations to them."

"Now, now," Mr. James said soothingly, getting up from his chair and going over to her. "I won't have you be upset. Who has upset you, darling?"

"Darling?" the earl asked.

"Darling?" her mama said.

"A figure of speech," said Mr. James. "No, no, it isn't. Sally, it is you who must come into the garden with me."

"Not without me," Mrs. Eckle said stoutly, at the same time jerking her gold-and-green turban down more firmly over her hair.

"I think I'll stay here," Sally told Mr. James sadly.

"We'll talk, though. Tomorrow. Do not forget that we must do that tomorrow."

Sally sighed. "As though I could."

That made four people who planned to talk, Regina thought, counting not only herself and Lady Sanding but also Mr. James and Sally. How peculiar everything seemed.

The earl put his hand on Regina's arm. "Yes?" she asked.

"Mr. James called your friend 'darling,' " he said.

"I know it. He is a very affectionate person."

The earl, who had been looking relieved, moved off a bit. "Is that so? Has he been affectionate to you?"

Perhaps it was the hysteria no one had let her vent. Perhaps is was the general mood of the evening. In any case, not knowing why, Regina said, "Of a certainty. We are engaged to be engaged, after all."

The earl scowled. "I thought you'd got that nonsense out of your head. You aren't right for him, you know."

Regina's large brown eyes gazed into his. "I believe we had this same conversation sometime before, my lord. Yes, and I asked you who was right for him, and then I asked you who was right for me. As I remember it, your answers were not satisfactory."

Was he going to say what she wanted to hear this time? Regina leaned closer. The earl's nostrils flared as though once again he was getting a heady whiff of her perfumes. "I—"

"Regina, sit up straight," roared her drunken papa.

Slowly Lady Sanding rose from the table. She came around to where Regina's papa was sitting. "Excuse me," she said to the anonymous lady. "I must say something to Mr. Hammond. Mr. Hammond, it is you and I who need to talk."

It was at that point that Mr. Hammond banged his fist on the table and stood. "You are right. Something must be done," he said, swaying. "Everything is at sixes and sevens. What is more—forgive me, Lady Sanding—we all seem to be acting like fools tonight."

~Chapter 10

REGINA'S BEAUTIFUL FACE went pink with embarrassment. "Sit down, Papa, do," she said in an attempt to hush Mr. Hammond. "We all know what you mean."

"I do not," said the widow he had brought to their table.

As Mr. Hammond opened his mouth to explain, the earl went over to him and took his arm. "Come into the next room with me a minute, Hammond. I want to tell you about a new gaming hell I recently discovered in London. You would like it."

Mr. Hammond's mouth closed, and he went off willingly with the earl.

Regina smiled gratefully at the earl's back. She would have to thank him later for his help and apologize for having made him believe that she was still affianced to his uncle. Meanwhile she remained at the table, toying with her food, as did everyone else except the inquiring widow.

"He's right," said Mr. James in an unexpected outburst. "Everything is all to pieces—and wrong, wrong, wrong! Miss Hammond, may I speak with you privately tomorrow, too? I really must, you know."

Good God, was he going to propose to her again? But how could he? It was as plain as anything that he was in love with Sally. If Regina had thought her peace was cut up before, she now knew that "before" was a summer idyll compared with what she had to look forward to.

She was correct. The rest of the evening was decidedly worse, the *worst* thing being that the earl did not return to their table after escorting Mr. Hammond from the room.

Instead, of all things, he told the older man that he had another engagement and went off.

"Do you think that Mr. James will talk to you first, or to me first?" Sally asked Regina later that night when the two girls were alone in their bedroom, sitting hunched up on the bed in their fine lawn nightrails.

"I do not know," Regina said wearily.

"What do you think Mr. James wants to talk to you about?"

"I do not know that, either," Regina said, even though she was afraid that she did.

"Do you think that he is going to ask your permission to wed me?"

Regina gave her an irritable look, created by nerves as much as the lateness of the hour and the exhaustion that accompanied it. "Why should he? I am not your papa."

"No, I don't have one," Sally replied, making Regina feel like a low person.

Regina patted her hand. "I just don't know. Maybe it is something like that."

She was not merely saying the words for Sally's benefit now. It was plausible that Mr. James had some such thing in mind. After all, he did have a sort of obligation to her and would hardly toss her aside without explanation. He was too kind, too much the gentleman to do any such thing.

Sally stuck out her right foot and studied her toes. "What would it mean if he spoke to me first, and then to you, do you think?"

Regina shrugged. "I cannot imagine."

"It could be that he will ask me to marry him and then ask you to release him."

Regina nodded her head. "That is possible."

"Or it could be that he will ask you to release him first and then ask me to marry him . . . or—"

"Stop!" Regina said. "That is probably what it is. Does he know that you want to marry him?"

Sally stared at her, a look of despair on her face. "I don't think so. We never talked about anything like that." Her face wrinkled up. "He might not want to ask you about me and him and you at all. He might want to ask you why you cannot get along with the earl and then ask me what it means that I can.'' She finished this thought by bursting into tears.

Although Regina did not join her friend in her exhibition of lachrymosity, she thought she probably felt just as bad. ''Shush,'' she said while she stroked and patted Sally's back. ''It will be all right. You'll see.''

Surprisingly Sally quieted and soon was fast asleep. Regina was not so lucky, and it was a very tired young woman who saw the dawn come up and heard the birds greet it with bursts of song.

A breakfast shared with Sally and Mrs. Eckle did not make matters any better. ''Wasn't the Burnhams' ball strange?'' Mrs. Eckle asked.

Both girls nodded.

''I thought Mr.—'' She broke off, looked at Regina, then gave a self-conscious smile and subsided. Still Regina knew that Mrs. Eckle had been about to say something derogatory about Regina's papa.

The girl could hardly blame her. He had not behaved well the previous evening. Indeed, no one had.

''Mr. James called you 'darling' last night. I wonder what he wishes to talk to you about,'' Mrs. Eckle asked her daughter in an abrupt change of conversation.

Looking as though she hadn't given the matter any thought, Sally shrugged her narrow shoulders.

Mrs. Eckle was not put off. ''When are you going to speak with him?''

''Ah . . . why do you ask, Mama?''

''Why do I ask? Because I mean to be there with you, of course.''

''Oh. In that case, I don't believe we will have a talk.''

Regina stood. ''Would you and Sally like me to leave you, Mrs. Eckle?''

''Why?'' Mrs. Eckle asked, then gasped. ''I'm so sorry; I forgot that he is more or less your affianced husband.''

Regina shook her head. ''He isn't really.''

''He isn't?'' Mrs. Eckle repeated, raising her light brows. ''Has he refused to pick up the handkerchief after all?''

''I never did drop it,'' Regina said. ''I am not interested in Mr. James as a husband, and he is no longer interested in me.''

Mrs. Eckle looked shocked. ''Can that be true? Then why are we still at Fairways?''

Regina did not answer. For her part, Sally tapped her mouth nervously a few times before saying, ''That is a good question, Mama.''

''Does your papa know?'' Mrs. Eckle asked Regina.

Regina shook her head.

''We must leave tomorrow, if not today. It would not be right for us to stay any longer.''

Sally pushed back her chair and stood. There was a look of defiance on her flushed face. ''I won't go, Mama. I'm not yet ready to leave.''

''Why ever not?'' asked Mrs. Eckle, sounding bewildered and worried. ''Oh, no. Do not tell me that you are secretly in love with the earl. I was afraid of that. Do you remember the day you asked me to meet you at the gazebo, and when I did, the earl and Regina were there? I had the strangest feeling then that you were enamored of him. Was I correct?''

Sally hung her head and did not answer.

Her mama shook her own head in a gesture of despondency. ''I must inform you, daughter, that he will never return your feelings. He is a sophisticated man about town, one, moreover, who is used to having Incomparables drop into his lap like ripe plums. Besides, from what I've heard, he has no intention of marrying for years and years, if ever.''

''That means nothing to me,'' Sally replied, ''but you had better not talk that way in front of Regina.''

Mrs. Eckle wrung her hands. ''Why not?'' Not giving Regina a chance to reply, she said, ''Between the two of you, you will drive me mad. What is wrong with you girls?''

Neither answered, forcing Mrs. Eckle to come to her own

conclusion. "You're nervous," she said, "because it is nearly time for you to return to London for the season. It is almost past time."

"Not for me," Regina said.

Mrs. Eckle's look of chagrin changed to horror when her only child said, "Not for me, either."

"Sarah, I do not know what you are talking about. Of course, you must return to town."

"Mama," Sally said gravely, "please sit down. I have something to tell you, but first you must promise me not to make a to-do over it."

"You're breeding," her mama cried, "both of you. I have been the worst sort of chaperon. Regina, your papa will kill me."

Sally gave her a puzzled look. "How could we be breeding? We are not married."

With a sigh of relief, Mrs. Eckle quickly said, "Never mind; I made a mistake. What do you want to tell me?"

"I . . . I am in love with Mr. James, and—isn't it amusing? I do not even know his first name."

"Mrs. Eckle frowned at her only child. "Severn. Don't say stupid things, Sarah."

"Severn?" Sally repeated absently. "What does that mean? It doesn't matter. I am not being stupid—or, probably I am, but at least I am being honest. I love him, Mama, I do, and I will not leave Fairways until I get him to love me, too."

"But what about Regina and her papa? Surely he must still believe she is affianced to Mr. James."

"I cannot help that," Regina said in an offhand manner. "My papa should know I don't want to wed Mr. James. I never did."

Mrs. Eckle's eyes were darting about in her head, giving her the appearance of a shocked squirrel. "But there is your come-out, Sarah. You must not love anyone until you've had that."

"I don't want a come-out, Mama; that is what I've been trying to tell you. Besides, it is too late to say to me that I must not love Mr. James. I already do."

Mrs. Eckle gave her daughter a haunted look. Then, ignoring the latter part of Sally's statement, she said, "Don't want a come-out. You've got to have one. I have been planning for it since you were born. Besides, Mr. James is so much older than you."

"That doesn't matter," Sally said with finality.

Her mama hesitated, then said, "I know this is an odd thing to say, but do you think you are drawn to him instead of someone younger because you do not have a papa?"

"That is an odd thing to say. Besides, I don't remember Papa. Is Mr. James like him?"

Mrs. Eckle's mouth twitched as though she might have laughed if she hadn't been so distressed. "Not a bit," she said. "Your papa was wild and exciting, rather like the earl. Mr. James is very nice, but I don't believe anyone would say he is wild and exciting."

"I think he is," Sally said firmly. "What is more, I want him to kiss me and love me and—"

"Sarah, that will be enough of that sort of talk. Perhaps you *should* get married right away, and not wait for your come-out after all."

"To Mr. James?"

"Yes, to Mr. James, if he will have you."

Sally threw herself at her mother, almost upending the poor woman. "Oh, Mama, I love you."

Mrs. Eckle adjusted her frivolous-looking cap, which her daughter had half knocked off her head. "Thank heavens for that. We will just have to see what we can do. Now, Regina, it is your turn. Please think of me as your mama, too, and tell me what is wrong."

"I can't talk about it," Regina said.

"You can't? Are you certain that you are not breeding?"

Regina blushed. "Uh . . . do kisses make you have babies?"

"No. Don't tell me he kissed you."

"I won't if you do not wish me to, but he did," Regina said with a melancholy smile. Remembering was painful.

Sally threw out her arms. "Oh, Regina, he didn't! What was it like?"

"That will be enough out of you, young woman," said her mama, giving her daughter's arm a pinch.

"Mama, if I am going to marry Mr. James, I need to know how it is to be kissed by him."

Regina stared at her. "I've never been kissed by Mr. James. It was the earl who kissed me . . . uh . . . several times."

"He didn't!" Sally said in accents of awe. "Several times. Isn't that wonderful!"

"I cannot cope with this just now," said Mrs. Eckle, picking up a piece of toasted bread and fanning herself with it. "Girls, I want you to remember that you are ladies. Regina, I want you to stay away from the earl."

"That won't be any problem," Regina said sadly. "He does not care for me."

"Keep that in mind, my dear. Keep in mind also that you are from a fine family. Do not let thoughts of the earl cause you to forget that and bring disgrace upon yourself and your papa."

"Yes, ma'am," Regina replied because she knew that was what she was expected to say.

Mrs. Eckle nodded, apparently satisfied. A short while later, to Regina's relief, she left the girls alone.

"I still cannot believe you are fond of the earl," Sally said as soon as her mother disappeared from view.

"I'm not. That is what your mama said. Actually I adore him."

"I'm so glad. He is very handsome—and somewhat difficult, I think. Don't you just love difficult men?"

Regina did not answer that question, but instead asked one of her own. "I cannot understand how you can say you are attracted to difficult men when it is Mr. James you've fallen in love with. No one would say that he is difficult."

"He doesn't need to be," Sally answered stoutly. "I am exciting enough for both of us."

Regina frowned. "Does that mean that I am not exciting?"

"No—for the ordinary male, you would be. Your looks

alone make you that. For the earl, though, you are probably quite restful.''

Regina was not certain that she liked being so described. Being considered restful did not seem particularly appealing to her. ''I am?'' she said doubtfully.

''Certainly. He's known gobs of beautiful women, I'm sure—like Lady Sanding. What makes him want to kiss you, I'll wager, is that you aren't a stunner inside.''

''Thank you very much!''

Sally rushed over and hugged her friend. ''I don't mean that. I'm making a mess of this. I never can explain things. Do you want me to continue to try?''

''Yes. In fact, I insist.''

''Very well. Let me see. Even though you are extraordinary outside, which I am certain he likes very well—why wouldn't he?—inside, you are simply a nice, calm person— usually, except when you get mad at the earl. You love animals and the countryside and rain and flowers and all that sort of thing. You are a loyal friend, too. Who could ask for more?''

Sorrowfully Regina said, ''I believe the earl could.''

''Oh.''

''What do you mean, 'Oh'?''

''I mean, oh, Mr. James is here. My mama has come back as well.''

''Oh,'' Regina said.

Mr. James followed Mrs. Eckle into the room. He was dressed in riding clothes, and for a minute Regina hoped he meant to ask her and Sally to ride with him. Instead, however, he said, ''With your permission, Mrs. Eckle, Miss Hammond, are you ready for our little talk?''

Looking as though she were about to face her execution, Regina nodded and stood.

''Where do you mean to take her?'' Mrs. Eckle asked with a scowl. ''I hope you do not think to go off with her unchaperoned.''

''I'll go with them,'' Sally said, jumping up precipitously and spilling a cup of coffee on her dress as she did. She sank back embarrassed into her seat.

Mr. James tightened his jaw and said, "We are going outside, madam, if that is all right with Miss Hammond." Regina nodded. "However, we will walk just a little distance from the windows, in full view of anyone who wants to look. We will not need a chaperon. Come, Miss Hammond. Miss Eckle, I am sorry."

What was he sorry for—the things he meant to say to Regina or the fact that Sally had spilled her coffee? Regina grabbed a piece of her pretty blue muslin dress between her agitated fingers and proceeded to mangle it. She did not think to refuse Mr. James, however.

Once they had put some distance between themselves and the house, Mr. James turned to her and put a hand on her arm as a gesture to stop.

"Listen to the birds," Regina said tensely. "They are very melodic, are they not? I can recognize a linnet and a—"

His hand tightened on her. "Never mind the birds, Miss Hammond. Listen to me, please."

Regina looked up at him bravely. "Very well."

Mr. James took a deep breath. "Good. Miss Hammond, I have done you much wrong; I do not, and do not wish to, deny it. I have done it from the first."

"Really? What sort of wrong?"

"I fear I put pressure on your papa to let me be betrothed to you; I confess it. I should not have done that."

"You are too harsh on yourself," Regina said with an anxious smile. "Besides, wrongs can be righted."

Mr. James wiped his hands upon the sides of his breeches and gave Regina an imploring smile. "That is what I hope to do now, right a wrong. Miss Hammond, when I first saw you, I was struck by your beauty, yes, and your youth as well. Selfishly I wanted to possess them, just as Paris wanted to possess the exquisite Helen—and you know what came from that!"

Paris? Helen? What was he talking about? "Hmm," she said.

He put out his hands and shifted them, as though

balancing weights. "Of course, if I had not, I never would have met . . . uh . . . everyone else."

Nor would she have met the earl. "That is true," she said more genially than she might otherwise have done—although, on second thought, meeting the earl was not exactly an unmitigated blessing.

"I should not digress," Mr. James continued. "It was then that you and I became more or less affianced, and are still more or less betrothed, in a sense, because we have never gotten ourselves not betrothed. I hope you understand what I am saying."

He had not been especially easy to follow, but she had managed. The important thing, however, was not what he'd said but what she should say to make the situation less difficult for him. "We were never formally betrothed," she said. "No announcement was sent to the papers; therefore we do not have to declare that our betrothal is at an end. That is what you want, isn't it, to end it between us?"

"If you wouldn't mind, dear Miss Hammond."

She nodded.

Mr. James's brow furrowed. "But still there is the problem that everyone here thinks that we are affianced, or about to be," he said.

Regina sighed. "I am not certain of that. I told Sally, Miss Eckle, that is, and her mama that I do not mean to marry you. I like you, but I never wanted to marry you, you know," she added softly.

Mr. James wrung his hands. They were very nice hands, Regina thought, slender and pale and small, a gentleman's hands, unlike the encroaching hands of that buccaneer the Earl of Audlin. "What did Miss Eckle say?" he asked in a breathless voice.

If Mr. James could talk so obliquely about being not betrothed, Regina could talk the same way about being not miserable. "She was not unhappy," she said.

"Not unhappy? *Not,* you say? That is good news." In an ecstasy of hope, Mr. James got down on his knees in the grass. "My dear Miss Hammond, do you think this means . . . ?"

Gently she put her hands into his. Her smile was beatific. "Dear Mr. James, she loves you. You must know that. And you love her."

He covered her gloved hands with kisses. "I do," he said. "I do. I love her." Rising a bit awkwardly, he gave her a huge hug and an affectionate kiss. "Thank you, Miss Hammond. I will not forget this. And if ever I can do anything for you, or your father, please do not hesitate to tell me and know that not only will you get that help, but also it will be a secret between us. If you don't mind now, I'd like to return to the house, first to talk to Miss Eckle's mama, and then to Miss Eckle. To Sally," he said with a wide smile.

Regina nodded, then watched him stalk away in the wrong direction. After a bit he stopped, waved once a trifle sadly at her as though bidding farewell to beauty, changed course, and headed in the correct direction.

From a window of the blue saloon, the earl, Sally, and Mrs. Eckle watched him as well. Indeed, they had been watching him and Regina for the last fifteen minutes or so. "If he weren't my uncle, I'd shoot him dead," the earl muttered. The ferocious look on his face suggested he meant every word.

"Shoot me instead," Sally cried, sinking to the carpet. "I have nothing left to live for. I've lost my dearest friend and my dearest . . . dearest."

"Get up, Sally," said her mama. "We must tell the maid to get our things ready."

Sally looked at Mrs. Eckle through tear-blurred eyes. "You can't expect me to want to go visiting now, Mama. My heart is broken."

"Visiting? Certainly not. We are leaving this place."

"Leaving Fairways? Leaving Mr. James?" The trickle of tears turned into a torrent.

Mrs. Eckle grabbed her daughter's hand, after first bestowing a look of loathing on the earl. "You have turned into a real watering pot, Sarah, and I do not like it. Stop it or I shall be forced to slap you."

Sally hiccuped, then subsided.

"Good," said her mama. "Now, you cannot expect to stay here any longer after this . . . this . . . you know. Haven't you any pride?"

"I don't know," Sally said, but her back stiffened. "Yes, I do, and you are right. Do you have a handkerchief?"

The earl leaned over and handed her his.

Sally rose, her back ramrod straight. "We shall leave. First, however, I want to tell Mr. James and Miss Hammond what I think of them. No," she added after a pause, "I do not. In truth, I do not wish to speak to either one of them ever again."

"Well, I do," the earl said. "I mean to blister both their ears. Then I will never speak to them again."

Sally nodded and handed him his wet handkerchief. She walked toward the door, but stopped when there was a knock upon it, followed by the entrance of the butler. He held a silver salver with a number of cards upon it. "Gentlemen and some ladies asking for Miss Eckle and Miss Hammond," he said.

Sally ran back to the earl and snatched up the handkerchief. She used it to scrub at her face. Then, ignoring her mama, she turned and seated herself upon a pale blue sofa. "Show them in, please," she said, her lips quivering only a little.

Thus it was that when Mr. James tracked Sally to the blue saloon, he found himself not only with her but also with a number of rather noisy young people, many of whom he recognized from the previous evening. "Welcome, welcome," he said, his joyousness overflowing. "I am happy that you are here."

"I shouldn't wonder," Mrs. Eckle said caustically. "That way you do not have to face the people you have injured."

Mr. James looked puzzled. "Injured? Why, what do you mean?"

"As though you didn't know." She showed him her back and addressed her daughter. "Sarah, are you ready to go?"

Sally's chin came out defiantly. "No, Mama, I am not. I am having too good a time with my friends."

"I have something about which I wish to talk to you," Mr. James whispered in her ear.

"I don't want to hear it," she whispered back.

"Oh, but you will. I am sure of it—or very nearly sure."

Sally's freckles stood out like little anthills on her pale face. Her sandy brows lowered, giving her a menacing look. "Is it about Regina Hammond?"

"In part, yes."

"Go away," Sally whispered. "I have no intention of speaking to you."

Looking more puzzled than shattered, Mr. James moved over to where his nephew stood. "Is something wrong with Miss Eckle? She does not seem herself."

The earl stepped back as though in fear that his uncle would pass the plague onto him. "Nor do you," he said.

"I? What is that supposed to mean?"

"It means," the earl replied with heavy emphasis, "that you are behaving like a fool. But don't say later that I did not try to warn you, and stop you, too."

"I won't," Mr. James said in a conciliatory voice, privately convinced that Sally and the earl had gone mad while he'd been outside with Regina. "I will prove you wrong, though," he could not stop himself from adding.

The earl sneered. "Is that so? I beg to disagree. I think you will find only sorrow with that young female. I pity you, Uncle."

Mr. James frowned at his nephew. "You are beginning to anger me, Steven. I will not have you denigrate my future bride."

"Your bride!" The earl blanched. "I don't believe it." When his uncle did not reply but only glared at him, the earl said, "I suppose that I must wish you joy of her—but you won't have it. She is *not* for you." With those words, he headed for the door, pushing several people out of the way. No one demurred, probably because a single look at the furious expression on his face was enough to convince anyone that the earl, like a rabid dog, should be given a wide berth.

He started to walk toward the front door, meaning to find

Regina and give her the tongue-lashing of her life. No, on second thought, he would be gentle, commiserating, expressing sorrow for the mistake she had made that would ruin the rest of her life and that of his uncle. "Damn it," he said savagely, "no, I won't. I'll strangle her."

"Did you say something, Audlin?" Mr. Hammond asked. He and Lady Sanding had just come from the breakfast room and practically run into the earl. "I can't hear too well this morning. Can't see very well, either. Have the worst headache. Lady Sanding says I deserve it."

Lady Sanding took a careful look at the earl's face. "Come back inside the breakfast room," she said hastily to Mr. Hammond. "We can continue our talk there."

"I thought we'd got everything worked out between us," he said, not noticing that the earl had left them.

Lady Sanding gave him a slow, sweet smile. "We did, dearest one. Let us leave this hall and go find the others." Although looking confused because of their change of direction, Mr. Hammond followed obediently in her wake.

The earl, meanwhile, slammed out the front door. He peered around him but could not see Regina anywhere. He wondered if she had walked into the woods in order to feed her birds.

Choosing the path where he had once found her thus engaged, he walked rapidly along it. Then he stopped. Up ahead was his quarry, a lovely smile on her face, talking to a tiny wren perched on her hand.

How sweet she looked and how innocent. No one watching her now would realize that she was a little witch. But he knew. And she was soon going to be made aware of just what he thought of her.

Blue eyes narrowed, his black hair mussed from the restless movement of his fingers through it, he advanced along the path. The bird noticed him first. Quickly it flew away.

Regina looked up and then over at him, a dreamy look on her beautiful face. "I was hoping you would find me here."

"Were you?"

She blushed prettily. "I thought perhaps you might have talked to Mr. James and then decided to look for me."

"Did you? Why would I want to do that?"

Regina's dreamy look vanished, replaced by an expression of worry. "Is something wrong, my lord?"

"Wrong? Why should something be wrong?"

"Yes, that is what I asked you, and please do not answer me with a question."

He smiled. His smile made Regina shiver. "Very well, I will not. Instead I will give you a lesson."

A little afraid, she backed away from him. "What sort of lesson, my lord?"

He put out a hand to stop her. "Ah, now it is you who asks a question, but unlike you, I do not mind. Did you know that there are places in the world inhabited by savages who collect other people's heads? These savages are called, not surprisingly, headhunters."

Regina shuddered. "How awful."

"It is awful, isn't it? And so uncivilized. And yet—you may find this hard to believe–yet there are other people, so-called civilized people, who hunt heads, too, for their collections."

"No," Regina cried.

"Yes. And even more amazing, these so-called civilized head-hunting people of whom I speak are female."

Regina's expression changed from one of dismay to one of caution. "Is that so?"

"It is so; have I not said it? But wait, there is more. These females do not cut off their victims' heads, as the savages do. No, instead they get their victims to take off their own heads and give them to these women. Isn't that incredible?"

Regina's lips turned up in a pretense of a smile. "I must go, my lord. Mrs. Eckle is expecting me."

One of his hands clamped around her wrist. "Stay, Regina. I have not finished my lesson. Where was I? Oh, yes. Now, not all of these females are beautiful, as you might think. By and large, however, such women tend to be beautiful. Men are truly fools when it comes to female beauty."

"I wouldn't know," Regina said, narrow-lipped and a bit frightened. She was quite sure by now that the earl was not talking about headhunters but, in some indirect way, about her. He simply had not gotten to the heart of his attack yet.

What a fool she had been, convinced as she was that he would look upon her decision not to marry his uncle with favor. Instead he seemed as angry as though she had agreed to marry him after all.

"Take my word for it," he said.

Regina twisted her wrist, still within his grasp. At once he let her go. "Thank you for telling me about these people," she said. "I fear that I cannot stay to hear the rest, however. I must leave."

"No, Regina, you will not leave, not until I tell you what I think of you."

"I knew it. I knew you were not talking about savages, but about me. What I do not understand is why."

The earl's dark brows came down over his eyes, making him look fierce and not entirely in control of himself. "Your pretense of innocence offends me more than anything else you've done or said."

All of a sudden Regina grew angry. What a hypocrite he was. "From what I've heard, my lord, if there is anyone who has collected heads, as you call it, it is you. I am referring, of course, to female heads."

The earl's blue eyes widened. Then a self-mocking smile touched his lips. "You are right; I cannot deny it. Do you know what I am beginning to believe?"

"What, my lord?"

"I am beginning to believe that there truly is divine retribution, as the preachers promise; and if there is, Regina Hammond, you are undoubtedly its instrument, at least in my case. I'm sure I deserve it—but it hurts."

Slowly Regina shook her head. "I do not understand you at all, my lord. I thought you'd be pleased that I do not mean to marry your uncle."

"Not marry my uncle." He stared at her, a stunned look on his handsome face. "Is that what you said?"

He hadn't known about it after all. She nodded and waited for his smile of approval—and waited some more.

~Chapter 11

"SAY SOMETHING!" SHE shrilled at him. "Say that you are pleased by what I've told you."

As soon as she uttered those words, she was sorry. The earl did not seem the least bit pleased. What was wrong? If nothing else, he should have been delighted that she was not affianced to his uncle. It was what he had wanted from the first time he'd met her, wasn't it?

"You've changed your mind and decided to cast off my uncle, haven't you?" he said disapprovingly.

Regina's hands clenched so as to keep herself from striking Lord Audlin. Would the man always think everything was her fault?

No, she thought, he wouldn't. Instead he would forget about her completely, or if he thought of her at all, every now and then, she would simply be someone he used to know. Thinking this gave her no joy.

"I did not change my mind," she said coldly. "I feel exactly the same about Mr. James as I did yesterday and the day before and as I always did."

"Yes, that you do not love him but you mean to marry him anyway."

"You are not listening," she said, sounding angry now. "I will not marry him, and he does not want to marry me. It was a mutually agreed-upon thing."

There went the earl's eyebrows again. "I'd have to have been born yesterday to believe that," he said.

"But it is true. I do not wish to marry him—I never

165

did—and he does not want to marry me, not anymore. He told me so.''

The earl's aristocratic face took on a stubborn look. ''You must think I am naive indeed, Miss Hammond, to believe that he no longer wants you. That isn't possible. Besides, he told me—'' He broke off. ''What's the use?''

She supposed it was flattering in a way that he could not conceive of his uncle no longer being in love with her, but she did not need that sort of flattery. ''He loves Sally Eckle,'' she said.

The earl began to laugh.

Regina glowered at him. ''What are you doing? Stop that. I haven't said anything humorous. He loves her, I tell you.''

Although the earl stopped laughing, his mouth kept twitching up at the corners in a smile. ''Are you trying to make me believe he would prefer her over you? That is the stupidest thing I've ever heard.''

Regina sighed. ''It is true, my lord. He loves her.''

''No. You must mean that he likes her. I can believe that at least. She is a nice person, when she is not peering.''

''Thank you for that,'' she said sarcastically. My, he was a stubborn man.

The earl gave her a wary look. ''What does this mean?''

''To whom? I do not understand your question.''

''I'll ask another. Why did my uncle kiss you and kiss your hands when the two of you were outside together?''

''You were spying on us. Shame!'' Regina said scornfully.

The earl straightened, making him seem even taller and more formidable than before. ''It was not necessary to spy, Miss Hammond. You and my uncle were carrying on for all the world to see. And all the world did see.''

Regina's expression became cautious. ''What are you saying, my lord?''

''I am saying that the fine show you and my uncle put on was seen not only by me, but also by your dear friend Sally and her mama. I have no doubt that they enjoyed it as much as I. I also have no doubt that they would believe your story about breaking it off with my uncle as little as I do.''

What was the use? He was bound and determined to place her in the wrong. Regina spun on her heel and began to walk away from him.

"Halt!" he said. Despite herself, Regina obediently did as she'd been ordered. With quick steps, the earl came up to her and faced her. "Ignore what I said before. Am I correct in supposing that you and your papa will be departing Fairways soon?"

Was he going, at last, to tell her not to leave him? Was he going to tell her that now that she was not committed to his uncle, he wanted her to be committed to him, forever? Was he going to tell her that he loved her and would do so all his nights and all his days? Or was he still determined not to marry her?

"Why should we stay here any longer now that I am not engaged to Mr. James?" she asked hopefully.

He hesitated. "I don't know. I suppose you do need to return to London for the season."

"I do not expect to take part in this season, my lord," she said quietly.

"Don't be absurd. Of course you will." When Regina shook her head, he said, "Where are you planning to go, then?"

"Go? I do not mean to go anywhere other than to our town house so that my papa may take up his usual life again."

He frowned. "Then why won't you take part in the season's activities?"

She was too proud to admit to him that her papa did not have enough money for a come-out for her; she could not humble herself before him so. Besides, truth to tell, a come-out did not interest her anymore; all she wanted was Lord Audlin. "I do not wish to discuss it," she told him.

His Lordship put his hand to her face and tipped up her chin. "I insist."

Regina had had enough. "Do not attempt to bully me, my lord. I have no intention of going over my affairs with you." She hesitated. "After all, you have no interest in my future."

If the situation had not been so painful, she might have laughed: the expression on the earl's face was that of someone who desperately wants to eat the rich, marvelous dessert offered him, but knows that shortly after he swallows it, it will make him sick. "I do, naturally," he said. "As a friend . . ."

Regina smiled humorlessly. "We are not friends, my lord."

The earl's mouth thinned. "You are right; we are not, and that is too bad, because I fear there is nothing else for us to be."

He had decided to pass up the dessert after all. His intentions, or lack thereof, could not have been clearer. He was not going to try to keep her there. He was not going to visit her in London. He had no idea of marrying her, although she could have sworn that he did not want anyone else to have her.

There was nothing she could do about any of it. She could not kidnap him or even propose to him. The choice was his, and he had made it. Her beautiful, dark-eyed face became suffused with sadness. "Good-bye, my lord," she said softly. She put her hand up to touch his cheek, then let it drop. "Good-bye."

Looking miserable, the earl stood there, not saying a word. He stood there and watched her walk away from him, until he could not see her anymore. "Damn," he said. "Damn, damn." Swinging around, he punched the tree next to him as hard as he could, for his pains acquiring scraped and bleeding knuckles.

Mr. James sat alone with Sally in the blue saloon, the guests having departed and Mrs. Eckle having gone to her room. Even though he hadn't managed to ask Mrs. Eckle for permission to address her daughter, he was determined to speak to Sally now. Rising from his wing chair, he walked toward her with outstretched hands and a huge, if nervous, smile on his face.

"What is it?" she asked, staring gloomily up at him.

His hands dropped and his smile began to fade. "I . . . I have something to ask you."

"If it is to be Regina's attendant when you marry her, I'd rather you did not ask me now."

Mr. James sat down beside her and turned her face toward him. "Miss Hammond and I? Why should you think that?"

"I was watching through the window," she said. "I saw you kiss her. I saw you hug her, too. What else is there to think?"

Mr. James reddened. "Certainly I cannot deny that I did those things. However—"

"I do not wish to hear your explanation, sir. It is none of my concern," Sally said with touching dignity. "Please go away."

Severn James's hands went about her wrists. "I won't," he replied, with an unusual display of determination. "I insist that you listen to me."

Sally shrugged. "Very well. Say what you have to say—if you must."

"I must and I will." He released her hands and sat back. "What you do not understand, my darling Sally, is that I was kissing and hugging your friend out of relief, because we decided mutually to dissolve our engagement to be engaged. I am free now—free to marry another."

She gazed hesitantly into his loving blue eyes. "Really? What other?"

"You, Sally, you," he answered, laughing.

Shock made her gape at him. "Ah . . . do you mean to tell me that you are giving up Regina Hammond for me? I cannot believe it. Why would you do that?"

"The answer is very simple," he said. "I love you."

"Do you really? Oh, Mr. James."

Severn James got down on one knee. "Miss Eckle . . . Sally . . . will you marry me?"

"Are you certain? Then, yes, I will," she said upon a sigh. "I will, Mr. James."

"And dare I hope that someday you will return my love?"

"Someday?" Sally said with a laugh. "I love you now, Mr. James. Indeed, I have loved you for some time."

Looking rather dazed, he got to his feet. "Is that true? We've been together such a short while. And even though I knew you liked me, I had the impression . . . more than an impression . . . that you were in love with my nephew."

"Never mind about that," she said with a careless sweep of her hand. "I don't love him anymore, and never did the way I love you. Would you like to kiss me, Mr. James?"

"Severn," he murmured. "And, yes. Yes, I would."

And so he did, not even the appearance of the astonished Mrs. Eckle upon the scene causing him to desist until she tapped him forcefully upon the shoulder.

"Mama," he said, causing Mrs. Eckle to cringe.

Regina returned to a house seemingly gone mad. The servants were assembled in the hall, with glasses in their hands; Mr. James, Sally, and Mrs. Eckle were there also, bunched together in a tight little group as though held to each other by invisible bands; and her papa and Lady Sanding were there, standing so close that their bodies touched at the hip. Only the earl was missing, and Regina knew where he was, having left him behind in the woods.

"What is happening?" she asked, although she had a very good idea of the answer.

Sally ran forward. "Regina, my dear friend, you must wish us happy. Mr. James and I are to be wed."

"I do wish you happy," she said before kissing Sally. Her felicitations were sincere, especially because now she could keep Sally as a friend; if she herself had married Mr. James, she felt certain their friendship would have ended.

Her other feeling, carefully hidden, she hoped, was sorrow, for herself. If only she could have announced her engagement to the earl, she would have been as happy as the others. Oh, yes, those others . . .

She turned now to look at her papa and Lady Sanding. "Is there something you two wish to tell me also?"

Her papa reddened slightly, then grabbed Lady Sanding's hand and held their two hands up together. "Her Ladyship and I mean to marry, too," he said. "What do you think of that, daughter?"

Some of what she thought she would never tell him, and hopefully, in time, her feelings of jealousy would disappear completely. "I wish you both happy, too, Papa," she said, trying hard to sound enthusiastic. She went over to them and kissed each of them.

"You are a good daughter," said Mr. Hammond, beaming at her. "Your turn will be next."

That was probable, eventually, since of the lot of them only she and Mrs. Eckle still remained unattached. Or perhaps it wasn't. The way she felt now, if she could not have the earl, which she couldn't, she never wanted to wed.

The next half hour was a torment to Regina. She wanted to go up to her room, fling herself upon her bed, and weep and weep. She did not want to stay there with the rest, pretending that she was in alt when, instead, her heart was breaking. She did not want to stay there fearing every minute that the earl would come in and she would have to look at him again and not cry.

Finally she was able to get away. Instead of going to her room, however, where Sally or Lady Sanding might have come in to talk to her, she fled to the woods. This time she looked for a different, gloomier part in which to hide. She was like an injured animal, wanting to be alone to lick its wounds.

She did not stop walking until she felt with some certainty that no one would be able to find her. Indeed, she was not convinced she'd remember how she had come to that place so that she could retrace her steps later. At that moment, however, she did not care. She was lost anyway, wasn't she?

She smelled damp earth and musty things like toadstools and other, nameless fungi. She heard a lone crow caw and a broken branch fall. She sighed and sat carefully upon a downed tree that looked as though it had been singed by lightning. If one's emotions could reveal themselves in physical ways, she thought, she'd probably look the same.

She was grieving, for Lord Audlin. Grief hurt; it made her

insides ache, especially her throat. Although she did not cry, it seemed to her as though she were crying within herself. No one else could feel her sense of loss and know the thing that was inside her that was like crying, but they were there.

She shifted her feet and looked back in the direction from which she thought she'd come. Then she screamed.

"Don't do that," said the earl. "You'll frighten the wood nymphs."

"You. What are you doing here?"

"I went back to the house," he said. "I . . . I talked with the others."

Regina's expression became inscrutable. "Is that so?"

"Yes, and after I got through all the congratulations, including those to your father and Lady Sanding, I asked for you. When it was discovered that you weren't in your room, I felt sure you had come out here again. It is what you always do, isn't it—when you are distressed?"

Regina shrugged.

"How do you feel about your father marrying Lady Sanding?" the earl asked baldly. "Were you surprised? Are you upset? The precipitousness of the thing, at least, must have shocked you."

Regina almost said something sarcastic in reply, but why should she bother? she thought. "If they will be happy, I will be happy," she said.

The earl looked as though he did not quite believe her, but then nodded.

"I have a question for you," she said. "How did you find me here?"

The sophisticated Lord Audlin had a boyish, half-embarrassed smile upon his face. "I'm afraid I followed you, followed your tracks, at any rate."

"I don't believe it."

"It's true," he said, walking up to stand next to her. "When I was young, and here on holidays, I used to tramp all through these woods, pretending that they were in North America and that I was an Indian scout. I was rather good at being a scout, I believe, and it appears that I still am. You did not know that anyone was back there, did you?"

"If I had known, I would have gone somewhere else."

The earl lowered his hand and stroked her dark, curly hair. "Would you? Why is that, Regina?"

She jerked her head away and then stood. "What happened to your hand?" she asked, looking at his cut and scratched knuckles.

"I bumped into a tree earlier. It is nothing. Are you going to answer my question?"

"The answer is simple," she said, smoothing her blue day dress while willing her fingers not to tremble. "I do not want to see you. There is nothing else for us to say to each other."

He shook his head. "Untrue. There are a number of things I meant to say to you before but somehow forgot to."

She wanted to tell him that she had no desire to hear them. She would not, however, lest he decide that she attached a great deal of importance to their former conversation. Although it was true, she did not want him to know that. She had her pride, if nothing else. "There isn't anything I want to say to you, my lord."

"Good," he said. "Then you can just listen to me." Taking hold of her arm, he more or less forced her to sit upon the log again. He took his place beside her. "I have resolved to go to London for the season."

If he had told her that before, she would have been thrilled. It would have meant that she might hope to see him sometimes in the months to come, especially since her best friend and next-door neighbor would be betrothed to his uncle. Now all his news meant was that she might have to experience the torment of seeing him now and again while knowing that she would never be anything to him; he would never let her be. Grief was replaced by anger. "Yes?" she said. "So?"

The earl's mouth fell open and color ran along his strong cheekbones. "You have slapped me in the face, metaphorically speaking. Why did you want to do that, Regina?"

"Miss Hammond," she murmured.

He stood, apparently as angry now as she. "Miss Hammond, Regina, imp, shrew, wretched child—what's the difference? You have deliberately insulted me, but I do not know why. I hoped you would be pleased that I would be in London and come to visit you, yes, and take you about . . . uh . . . now and then.''

Regina rose as well, feeling too much at a disadvantage so far below him. ''I fear you hoped in vain,'' she said, but her voice was not as convincingly cold as it had been. ''Besides, if you had bothered to remember, I will not be going about much. I am not going to have a come-out. I told you that.''

''There are other things to do,'' he said, also sounding less angry than he had been. ''One can go to see the beasts in the tower, go to the opera, and to the theater. And surely you will receive some invitations to balls and the like even if you do not have a come-out. Are you planning to become a nun, Miss Hammond?''

''That is an idea. I had not thought of that.''

''I am trying to be helpful. Your flippancy is uncalled for.''

''I am crushed by your criticism, my lord. Indeed, my heart is broken.''

He looked at her, his lips narrowed. ''Would that it were.''

''Why? So that you can add another head to *your* collection?''

Lord Audlin groaned. ''Never mind about my collection of heads. I do not want to hear any more about it. Yes, I know. I brought it up first. Now I'm canceling it, for eternity.''

''You are arbitrary, my lord,'' Regina said scornfully. ''You are arrogant, dictatorial, and tyrannical.''

He grinned at her. ''Yes, but with it all, I'm charming.''

''Oh, do you think so? I don't find you so.''

The earl rolled his eyes. ''Good grief, Regina. Cry off. I brought you something,'' he added.

''Brought me something? Is it another dolly? No? What is it? I don't want it.''

Lord Audlin smiled. ''You can't make up your mind

whether I should give it to you or not, can you? Isn't that just like a woman!''

"My lord, I *am* a woman. Besides, I can make up my mind. I don't want it.''

He raised his dark eyebrows. "Is that your last word?''

Regina hesitated. "No. Tell me what it is.''

He laughed. "Will you give me a kiss if I tell you?''

She frowned at him. "Certainly not.''

"Good, because I don't want one—see, two can play at that game. It is my lucky locket,'' he said before she could turn away from him.

"I don't understand,'' Regina said simply.

"Come sit down again with me, and I will show you.''

Regina hesitated, then shrugged her shoulders, and re-seated herself upon the burned log. The earl came down beside her. "Here it is,'' he said, taking out his gold watch chain. On it, in addition to his pocket watch, was a beautifully embossed gold locket, which he proceeded to remove from the chain.

"It's lovely,'' Regina said. "Where did you get it?''

"It was my mother's.''

"Ah.'' With care, she ran a finger over the raised surface of the locket. The design was that of two hearts, one partially superimposed over the other. "It's lovely,'' she repeated.

"Do you want to see what is inside?'' Regina nodded eagerly. Using his thumbnail, the earl pried apart the two halves of the locket, then spread them all the way open. One contained a curl of silky dark hair, the other a miniature of a small boy with blue eyes and regular features in a very handsome face.

"That's you,'' she cried.

His Lordship looked pleased. "Indeed, it is.''

"Is the lock of hair from your head as well?'' He nodded.

Regina examined both objects with reverence before saying, "I cannot accept this gift, of course.''

Lord Audlin frowned. "What do you mean, you cannot accept it. I am giving it to you.''

Regina shook her head. "It is too personal. It would not be proper."

"If I give it to you, it is proper," he said arrogantly. "I want you to have it."

"Why, my lord?"

"Why? Damn it, how do I know why? Wait, I do know. It has always brought me luck; that is why. I want you to have it for luck."

She smiled ruefully. "Do you think that I need some luck?"

"Not really," he said bitterly. "With your face, your figure, and your nature, you probably don't need another thing. I imagine you'll be snapped up this time as soon as you venture outside the house."

Regina drew a bit closer to him. "What is my nature, my lord?"

"Fishing for compliments, Regina?" He smiled. "Very well. You are bright and sweet and shrewish and unspoiled and good-tempered and snappish and generous . . . oh, and at least a dozen more things that should not go together and which contradict, if not cancel out, each other. Will you take the locket, Regina? I truly want you to have it."

She looked as though she could not make up her mind, which was nothing more than the truth. She wanted it because it contained the portrait of him when he was young. Loving him, she felt as though she had loved him from the day he'd been born, even though she had not yet been born herself then. She felt tenderness toward him not only for who he was but also for who he had been. She was nearly as much in love with the child he'd been as she was with his adult self. In addition, she *liked* the child more than she liked him at present.

She reached out her hand, pulled it back, and extended it again. Why shouldn't she have what she wanted, especially since that would be all she'd have of him?

He put the locket in her hand. "Thank you," he said.

She would not cry. She wouldn't.

His Lordship rose, then lifted her up beside him. "Will you give me a kiss to dream upon, Regina?"

Was he *trying* to make her cry? "Why, my lord?" she asked sharply. "Is that to be your payment for giving me your locket?"

"That was not nice, Regina."

She blushed and hung her head. "I'm sorry, but still I want to know why you want it."

His large shoulders moved inside his tight blue jacket. "Because I am a fool and a person who enjoys being cruel to himself."

"Why do you say that you are being cruel to yourself?"

His grin was self-mocking. "What else can I say about a mature man who begs to be tormented by an exquisite child whom he will not accept and cannot quite bring himself to reject?"

"You've already rejected me."

"I don't care what I've done. Kiss me, Regina. Kiss me until my head spins and I can't breathe and we're not in the woods anymore but a bright, hot place where we don't have any concerns. Kiss me until we are absorbed into each other and there is only us, not you and me with our separate needs and desires. If not, I'll kiss you."

Regina shivered. "I'm afraid."

"So am I," said the earl, taking her into his arms. The next minute they slid to the ground together.

The earl kissed her and kissed her again, until she was breathless. His kisses were hungry and hard; they made her open her mouth to his tongue and arch her body against him.

The earl put his hands on her waist, then slid them up to her breasts until the weight of them was heavy on the backs of his hands. Regina whimpered, not from discomfort but from a hunger of her own. She wanted more.

One of the earl's hands left her breast and traveled down her side, to touch her thigh. As he stroked it he pulled her dress up, inch by slow inch. Regina did not demur.

Suddenly the earl's hand stopped what it was doing. "What's the matter?" Regina whispered, slurring her words. She sounded as though she'd had too much to drink. "Don't stop."

"Regina," said the earl slowly, "I think I had better."

"Why?"

"Because . . ." He interrupted himself, then said in a lighter tone, "Regina, do we fully know what I am doing?"

"What?" she asked. "What do you mean?"

"I do not believe that we should go on with this—*although the devil knows I want to*," the earl muttered. He rearranged her clothing. "Sit up, Regina, do."

Her hair was a mass of tangled curls; her eyes were drowsy and dark; her smooth, pale skin was flushed. Taking his hand, she sat up and stared at him.

The earl looked nearly as disheveled as she—and far more wild. "I must really care for you," he said. "I've never wanted to go on making love more than I do now, and yet I've stopped."

Her mouth tightened. Her features seemed to snap together. "Of course you care for me," she said, "so why do you not ask me to marry you, my lord, and stop torturing us both?"

The earl's shoulders slumped. "It is very tempting, far more than you can realize. I do love you, you know. But, Regina, I do not wish to marry, not even you, not now. The world offers much and there are still too many things for me to do. To name but one thing, now that Napoleon is defeated, I will be able to travel to the Continent again."

"Can you not do and taste and travel and still be married?" she asked, sounding genuinely perplexed. "I do not believe that being married means taking one's wife everywhere with one—although I daresay I should like to visit the Continent."

He ran a hand through his dark hair. "Forget about the Continent. You obviously do not know what you are saying. You'd never stand still for it; I can tell. No, whoever marries you will have to be—will want to be—married totally to you, month after month, year in and year out. I am not up for that yet."

"Well, no wonder," she said. "You make it sound so drab. Would that really be so terrible?"

"I . . . I'm not sure."

"Why has Mr. James decided to marry? Have you asked him?"

"No, but he is a different case. I do not believe he would be affianced now if it were not for his having seen you and fallen in love with your beauty. That seemed to open the floodgates for him, and now he is to marry your friend."

The two fell into an unhappy silence upon these remarks. After a few minutes His Lordship said, "I suppose we need to be going back to the house. People might talk otherwise. We wouldn't want that."

"You are very concerned about my virtue for a man who is wild and won't be ready to be tamed for years and years, if ever."

His eyebrows rose. "I am, aren't I? I think that you are bad for me, Regina—and I know that I am bad for you."

~Chapter 12

SHE LOOKED AT him gloomily. "I suppose that is the end of it then. There is just one question I must ask you before we part, my lord. I hope you will tell me the truth. Do you snore?"

The earl's mouth fell open; then he laughed in delight. "There you go, surprising me again. Why do you want to know that?"

Regina shrugged. "If I know you snore, I will feel better about not being married to you."

His blue eyes crinkled in amusement. "I must confess that I do, sometimes—although not all of the time, mind you. My valet and . . . uh . . . others have told me so. Do you snore?"

Regina seemed as taken aback by the question as he had been when she'd asked it. "I . . . I do not know. No one has ever said so. However, every so often I grind my teeth against each other in my sleep. My maid says the sound is unpleasant, and she's certain the pressure is not good for my teeth."

The earl spread out his hands, palms up. "There you are—I snore and you grind your teeth. It sounds disgusting, doesn't it? I do not know why anyone would wish to marry us."

Regina looked at him quizzically. "Is that all there is to marriage—going to bed, snoring, and teeth grinding?"

"Gad, I hope not. If it is, I won't ever want to marry."

Regina's lighter mood disappeared as quickly as it had arisen. Her eyes narrowed, and her lips screwed up. She looked like a beautiful child about to cry. "Tell me, my lord," she said grimly, "do you remember the night we all played Crambo and you recited a line from a poem? It went 'Since there's no help, come let us kiss and part.'"

The earl nodded, his expression suddenly wary.

"I found the poem in a book in your uncle's library the next day. I read it several times. Probably that is why I still remember it. Would you like me to recite it to you?" Without waiting for his answer, she said:

> "'Since there's no help, come let us kiss and part,
> Nay, I have done; you get no more of me,
> And I am glad, yea, glad with all my heart,
> That thus so cleanly I myself can free.'"

"Are you trying to tell me something?" the earl asked, tight-lipped.

"Yes, that I am through, and so is our association, my lord. You'll get no more of me. Please be kind, and go away now."

"Regina . . . ?"

"Then I will go away," she said. She rose from her seat on the log and began to run, ignoring his shouted orders to come back. She ran past trees and bushes, past patches of green grass and bare places, clumps of flowers and areas that looked as if nothing would ever grow there. She ran as though the hounds of hell were after her.

Since she had no idea which paths to follow, it was a miracle, or perhaps the good luck derived from the earl's locket, still clutched in her hand, that she found her way back to the house in short order. Once inside, she went to her room and did not come out again that day, even after a stern lecture about the responsibilities of being a guest delivered through her bedroom door by Mrs. Eckle.

Nor would she allow her friend to come in. Sally was informed that she would have to find another room in which to sleep.

Regina did not come out the next day, either. She must have felt better, however, because she ate everything on the trays left outside her door. She also tore up five notes from the earl, four of which inquired after her health and one of which offered to pay for a season for her. She pushed the pieces back under the door each time after she finished.

On the third day of her self-imposed seclusion, she allowed Lady Sanding to wheedle her way into her room.

Her Ladyship looked Regina over critically. "You don't appear to be happy, but you're still beautiful," she said.

Despite herself, Regina smiled. "Thank you. So are you."

"Yes, and it is such a help, don't you think?"

Regina hunched up her shoulders. "It hasn't helped me, Your Ladyship."

"Of course, it has, that and your appealing nature; you're one of a kind, my dear. Oh, did I tell you that the earl looks terrible?"

Regina seemed torn between worry and satisfaction. "Does he? What do you think is troubling him?"

Lady Sanding smiled. "I know what is troubling him. It is you. He is deep in love with you but cannot have you."

"That is not true," Regina said, clenching her fists. "He can have me—but only in matrimony. That is the problem. He does not wish to marry me."

Lady Sanding seated herself upon a pink chaise and adjusted her skirts. "He *thinks* he does not wish to marry you. In that, he is no different from most other men. The majority of them do not fall into our laps, you know. They need to be convinced that we are what they want. That is what you must do with the earl—convince him, I mean."

Regina frowned and shook her head. "I tried to do that yesterday, but he would not change his mind."

"Tell me, my dear, do you want to live the rest of your life, or even a year or two, without him? Love is not something that should wait, you know. If one waits, the other person may pass on to the next world before anything is made final."

It was not strange that a widow would have such a thought; however, that in no way made it less shocking. It led to only one answer to Lady Sanding's question; the answer was no.

Her Ladyship smiled pleasantly. "Good. Now tell me this—have you been doing anything to drive the earl mad?"

Regina gave her an appraising look. Apparently satisfied that Lady Sanding was not her enemy, and might even turn out to be a good friend, she smiled. "I believe I have, although I cannot say that I did those things deliberately."

"That does not matter. After a while they will become deliberate. You are young yet. What did you do?"

"I told him that I did not want him."

"That is good. One can never drive a reluctant suitor too mad. What have you been doing besides being indifferent?"

Regina brushed her hands against her pale blue skirts. "I've thrown his words back in his teeth."

"Excellent. What else?"

"I've turned down his offer to help me financially so that I might have a season. Besides the impropriety of it, I do not want him to do anything that might serve as a sop to his conscience."

Lady Sanding nodded. "You are very wise. I don't believe I will have much to teach you. Of course you could mention when next you see him that another person besides him wanted to help launch you. He will be jealous."

"Another person?"

"Yes. I mean me, but you needn't reveal that. Tell me, what do you plan to do to the earl next?"

Regina got up from her chair and walked over to stand in front of a handsome pink marble fireplace. Her optimism and enthusiasm seemed to desert her. "I do not know if there will be anything next since I have made him believe that I do not want him anymore—and if I were sensible, that would be true."

Her Ladyship moved her feet as though she planned to arise as well. All she did, however, was settle back more firmly against the cushions. "No, no. Being sensible isn't any fun. You must want him with all your being."

Regina hung her head. "I'm afraid I do," she said faintly, "whether I will or no."

"Never be ashamed of desiring a man," her unlikely mentor said slowly, "unless he's a groom or a footman. And don't be ashamed even then if you can handle matters discreetly. The point is to achieve the unconditional surrender of the man you desire."

Regina studied the beautiful blond woman sitting near her. "Did you achieve the earl's unconditional surrender when you wanted it?"

"Child, child, you do not have much tact, do you? Oh, well, I suppose you'll acquire some as you age. What you need to realize is that truth is not always a good thing. Indeed, I would go so far as to say that it is hardly ever a good thing. Tact is much better."

She grimaced at Regina. "Oh, dear, I just had a horrible thought. If you marry the earl, I will be his mama. Do you suppose I will go to hell for . . . uh . . . previously having known him?"

"I—"

"Don't answer that. You might say something tactless again."

Her Ladyship's green eyes narrowed. "Never mind about me and him anyway. That is history. Do you know what I believe? I believe that even if you do nothing, Steven will soon come to realize that he cannot live without you. However, it would be much more fun to do something. Well, will you take a chance and do something to gain your ends?"

"The earl once said that I should take chances. Perhaps I will if I can think of something to do."

"I can," said her soon-to-be mama. "Here is my plan. You shall lure him into a room with you, and I will lock you both in. Later your papa can 'discover' you together, being quite agreeably naughty, I hope. That part will be up to you. Well, what do you think?"

"I won't do it, not any of it," said Regina, looking horrified. "I won't."

Lady Sanding sighed wearily. "Very well, if you feel strongly about trickery, we won't try to get him to compromise you. Don't ever say that I did not attempt to help you, however.''

''I won't,'' Regina said, sliding limply into another chair. She scrutinized Lady Sanding's face. There was an excitement about it that suggested Her Ladyship had not given over on her idea of trapping the earl. Regina would have to be very careful. Otherwise she might find herself tied to a man who would never trust her again and never forgive her; she had seen his bitter reaction to Sally's similar machinations. As much as she loved the earl, she would rather not see him anymore than live in such a relationship with him.

While Regina was discussing the earl with Lady Sanding, the earl was in the library thinking about her. He was thinking of the fact that Regina had torn up all of his notes. It did not take a savant to realize that she'd meant it when she said she wanted nothing more to do with him.

The earl felt that he still had a bit of time left, however, in which he could change her mind about him if he wished. What he needed to decide was whether or not he wished it.

The decision was not an easy one to make. It would have consequences, one of them being that if he determined to marry her, he would have to give up his freedom. As he'd told her previously, she was not the sort to elicit, or accept, a halfhearted relationship. No, whoever loved Regina would love her body and soul.

He knew he wanted her body, of course, as she did his. Their passion for each other was irrefutable.

But did he want her soul, and was he willing to give her his?

He seated himself upon a leather sofa and stretched out his long legs in their well-fitting breeches. He lowered his eyes to stare at his shiny black boots and the gold tassel that adorned each one. Then he pulled in his legs and leaped to his feet. He was too restless, too unsettled, to sit still. He began to pace back and forth across the Turkey carpet.

Should I? Shouldn't I? Should I marry Regina Hammond? Should I give up my bachelorhood? Should I make her exclusively mine for the rest of our lives?

He remembered the first time he'd met her. It was at her

London town house, where he'd gone to tell her that she must not marry his uncle. Unfortunately his words had had the opposite effect on her from what he wanted. Pigheaded little thing, he thought with a smile.

Then there had been the time he'd bested her at archery. She hadn't accepted her defeat very well, to understate the matter. Nor had she been best pleased when he'd done better than she at ducks and drakes. Although feminine to the bone, she could be as proud and strong-willed as any man.

There were other memories, too, of Regina in a field of flowers with the sun caressing her hair and skin; Regina laughing in the stream, unaware that her wet clothing revealed the beauty of her breasts; Regina beneath his body as they clung together in the woods.

There was one more picture that came into his mind, causing him to smile again. It was of Regina at the Burnhams' ball, telling him how she had added heliotrope to the rinse water for her hair and washed with soap containing otto of roses.

Little darling. For all her self-possession and rare beauty, she was a tender, innocent creature, and needed him. Did he need her? Of a certainty, he did. The question still was, how much?

He would see her one more time and make up his mind. His jaw tensed. His handsome face grew grave. Their next meeting would decide his future.

Alas for him, it did not start off very well. When Regina came out of her room finally, he was standing in the hall, watching her door. "What are you doing here?" she asked, sounding put out.

"That is a pretty dress," he said in a low voice, looking at her in her pink muslin as though she were clothed in a queen's robes. "But where is the locket I gave you?"

In truth, she had put it away so as not to be tempted to look inside at the miniature and be weakened. Of course, she did not mean to tell him that. Instead she started to make up some pert excuse for not wearing it, but found she could not do it; she did not want to wound him. "I do not have a proper chain for it here," she said. "I will find one for it when we return to London."

His look of relief made her glad she had listened to her heart. Unfortunately it also showed that she was still too vulnerable to his needs. She was not ready to face him after all. She started to return to her room.

The earl took several giant strides toward her. "You must come out, Regina," he said urgently. "It is not good for you to stay in your room. It is not good for any of us. We all miss you."

"Do you?" she could not help asking.

He drew her away from her bedroom door. "Yes, especially some of us. Will you come down the stairs with me? We can go into the morning room. It is empty, or was the last time I looked in there."

She still resisted him. "Why should we go there?"

"I believe you once said you liked it."

She smiled, pleased that he should have remembered something like that. "I do like it," she said, allowing him to place her hand on his arm.

The morning room seemed almost absurdly bright and cheerful looking after the gloom of Regina's bedroom; such an abundance of light did not suit her mood. She started to step out of it again.

"No, please," the earl said. "Let us stay here." When she did not demur, he said, "I want to explain why I offered to pay for a season for you. I have been speaking with the Eckles and my uncle. They say that you do not mean to have a season because your papa has had some financial reverses. I can understand about that."

Regina's face turned red. "Your uncle should tend to his own affairs," she said.

The earl took her hand. "I quite agree. Therefore, although he means to inform you that he'll pay the shot for your season, it is I who will pay for it."

"The devil you will."

"Regina!" The earl seemed truly shocked by her reference to the fallen angel.

"I don't care," she said, removing her hand from his arm. "I've already refused you once by tearing up your note. Besides, I do not want a season; and even if I did, you are the last person from whom I would accept help.''

''You are proud,'' he said.

''Proud? I would not say so. I am ashamed.''

He grimaced. ''I did not mean proud in the sense you seem to mean. That doesn't matter. What does is that you accept my offer, thereby affording much pleasure to me and your other friends.''

The tack he had just taken appeared to please him. ''Yes, to your friends. And not just pleasure. It would grieve them and me deeply if you were to stay at home these months.''

Regina muttered something.

''In addition,'' he said, ''your friend Sally told me that she could not be happy if you were not to accompany her to the various entertainments of the season.''

''She does not need me. She has Mr. James.''

''She does need you,'' he said. ''She told me so just a little while ago. I need you, too.''

She gave him a disbelieving look. ''Why?''

''Why do I need you?'' He hesitated. ''To keep up my skills in the waltz, of course. Do you remember how we danced together?''

She remembered every second of that time. If she lived two hundred more years, she thought, she'd never forget. ''I don't remember it at all.''

The earl looked vastly disappointed, but he soon rallied. ''That is why you need to go about,'' he said. ''It is a waste to forget what you've already learned.''

''I want to forget. You needn't worry, though. There is someone else, someone more acceptable, who has offered to pay my expenses if I change my mind. I am thinking of saying yes to that person's offer. I will be certain to let you know if I do. Now, why don't you go away?''

He frowned. ''Who is it?''

''That is no concern of yours, my lord.''

''Don't you care for me anymore?'' he asked.

''I don't suppose I do,'' she said, hoping that she was driving him mad rather than driving him off.

''But how could that be?'' His Lordship sounded genu-

inely puzzled. "It was not so long ago that you loved me."
He raised his hand. "There is no use in denying it. You did.
I know the look."

She gazed at him with distaste. "I'm sure you do. You've
probably seen it on any number of females."

Instead of replying to that, he said, "I've wondered how
it is that a woman who would die for you one day would,
after you've broken it off with her, want to kill you the next.
It's always seemed as though there should be a little more
constancy to feelings of love."

Regina raised her dark brows. "I hope you are not
including me among that group. I have never wanted to die
for you, nor do I wish to kill you. To say the truth . . ."
Here she put her right hand behind her back and crossed her
fingers. "To say the truth, I am indifferent to you, my
lord."

"Although young, Regina, you have a horrible tongue. I
shudder to think what you will be like when you are older."

"Why should it matter to you, my lord? We will not
know each other then."

But he wanted to know her then. He wanted to know her
when she and he were very old. Hadn't he decided that? He
needed to do something or he'd lose her forever.

"Did you hear something in the hall?" he asked. "Or
perhaps it was at the door. It sounded as though it might
have been there."

Regina paled. Was it possible that Lady Sanding had
locked them in together even after Regina had told her that
she must not? She started to walk toward the door.

"Never mind," said the earl, blocking her path. "I will
see if anyone is there." Regina held her breath while he
went toward the door. The earl put his hand on the knob and
turned. The door opened. The earl stuck his head out, then
looked at her and smiled. "There's no one there," he said
before he lazily kicked the door to behind him.

"Perhaps you should leave the door open now," Regina
advised.

"I would, except that I do not want the servants to hear
you scold me."

"If I promise not to scold you, will you leave it open?"

"You are certainly concerned about the door. Do you expect me to attack you? I won't, you know."

"It isn't that," she said.

The earl stared hard at her. "You are not usually so skittish. Is there something I ought to know, Regina?"

"Lady Sanding . . ."

"What about Lady Sanding?"

How could she tell him? How could she not? "Lady Sanding was . . . ah . . . thinking that if you and I were locked in a room together, we . . . I cannot finish," she said.

His Lordship's eyes were steely. "I can. She said that if we were locked in a room together, I would be forced to marry you. Isn't that correct?"

"She might have been joking," Regina said weakly.

"I doubt it. That was how she acquired her first husband. Tell me," he said when her only response to this news was to make a choking sound, "what did you say to her after she made this suggestion?"

"How can you even ask? I said no, of course."

To Regina's surprise, the earl did not seem to find her answer satisfactory. "Why? Would it be such a hardship to be married to me?"

"I do not understand you, my lord. You do not wish to marry. You told me so; don't you remember? Besides, I would not want to acquire a husband by trickery. And then there is the fact that you would hold me responsible for what she'd done and never forgive me. Isn't that so?"

"You think you know me so well," he murmured.

What sort of a remark was that? It seemed obvious to her now that she did not know him at all. She stared at him. "You cannot know what you are saying. If we were to be found here together like this, you could—you could be forced to marry me."

"I understand that better than you, my dear."

"Don't you care? You were furious when Sally tried to have herself compromised."

"Not for one minute have I ever mistaken you for Sally."

"What does that mean? Sally or me, you do not wish to marry. You told me so."

He gave her an appraising look. "And what about you? Do you wish to marry?"

"Certainly," she said, raising her dark brows. "Any normal girl does. If you do not do something about the door," she added with a sigh, "I shall."

"Very well, I will." He went to the door, fiddled with the latch, and then closed the door again. "I still do not want the servants to hear you," he said with a smile, "but I have ensured that Lady Sanding cannot lock us in together. Now, where were we?"

"I fear we were not anywhere, my lord."

The earl shook his head. "But, Regina, everyone needs to be somewhere. There is that noise again." Once more, he walked to the door. He eyed it, then turned the brass knob. The door did not open. "What is going forward, Regina?"

"She wouldn't. I do not understand," she said not very convincingly.

The earl gave Regina a long look, which made her increasingly flustered. "It seems simple to me. We are locked in here together. Are you sure this wasn't your idea?"

"How dare you! You had best stop insulting me, my lord."

He made her a little bow. "I apologize. I think that someone has decided to bring us together, whether we will or no, unless . . . Are you *certain* that this wasn't your idea?"

Regina glared at him. "My lord, I do not want to bring us together, and certainly not this way. If you believe for a minute that I meant this to happen, you are much mistaken. You need not worry, however. I will tell my papa that we were tricked. He will believe me. Besides, I shall refuse to marry you."

The earl gave her an odd look. "Do you dislike me as much as that? I think I would make you an outstanding husband, were I to put my mind to it. In fact, for you I cannot imagine anyone better."

"Oh-ho, and why is that?"

"Because I can overlook your strange little face and lumpy figure, your terrible temper and unloving nature. Indeed, I am oblivious to them. I am only interested in your scholarship and also your grasp of matters such as crop rotation, animal husbandry, and fertilizers."

Regina laughed, and thought how much she loved him. She could not imagine anyone better than he, either. But despite his words, he did not want to marry. "You never will put your mind to it," she said, "not for years and years, at any rate."

"I might. One can never tell about things like these. Indeed, I don't doubt that with some gentle persuasion, I might be convinced to consider it."

Regina stared at him. "What are you saying, my lord?"

"I am saying that I do not like other men hanging about you."

"That is no concern of yours. For all your talk, you do not want to marry me; so why can't you leave me alone?"

"Believe me, my dear, I wish I knew the answer to that, especially since I'm convinced that I *should* leave you alone. Regina?"

Here it was. He would tell her again that nothing could come of their relationship. He would tell her that he was fond of her, even more than fond, but none of that mattered. "What?" she shrieked.

The earl looked rather surprised, but not enough, apparently, to deter him from what he meant to say. "Regina, are you certain that you will not accept a season from me?"

Taken aback, she said, "Why should I?"

"I know you have hope of finding a husband this year. However, I don't believe you can expect to marry someone from our class if you do not have a come-out."

Her face hardened. "Perhaps I do not want someone from our class. Perhaps I want to marry a banker, who will love me and give me a large diamond ring and a chinchilla cape."

"What the devil is chinchilla? Is it that odd crimped-looking gray fur stuff?"

"It is, although it sounds hideous the way you describe it. I want a cape of it."

"I will buy you one, and a diamond ring."

"My lord, are you offering me a carte blanche?"

"No, you silly chit. I am offering you a season."

"And a chinchilla cape and a diamond ring? I don't see—"

"Drat it, Regina, neither do I. I must be asking you to accept something else, something other than a season and an ugly fur."

"What, then?"

"I suppose it must be me."

Regina drew in her breath. "What are you saying, my lord?"

"I'm saying that I want to be your husband, I suppose. The thing is, I can't leave you alone. My head tells me that I should, but I can't." Smiling, he threw up his hands. "I surrender, Regina."

There was a cautious expression on her face. "To what?"

"To my fate; to you, love; to marriage. Regina, will you marry me?"

Her dark eyes grew round with wonder. She stared at him, dumbstruck. "Why?"

"What do you mean why? You are supposed to say yes and fall into my arms."

Her heart was in her eyes. "I won't say anything until you tell me why you want to marry me."

"Regina, Regina," he crooned, "I love you."

"You loved me yesterday, my lord. You told me so. However, you did not ask me to marry you yesterday. You said you would not because there was still a whole world out there to taste and do things with and travel to. That world is still there."

"Must you remember everything I've said? For God's sake, Regina, don't start quoting poetry to me again. I couldn't bear it."

"I won't. But you must tell me what is different between yesterday and today."

"It is not complicated. Yesterday I was afraid."

"And today?"

"Today, I am terrified. Nevertheless I'm asking you, Regina—" He broke off to get down on his knees. "Will you marry me? Will you love me and bear my children and lead me around when I am old and feeble? Will you spend your life with me?"

She did not answer.

The earl raked his fingers through his dark curls. "For God's sake, Regina, put me out of my misery. Tell me."

"I'm thinking," she said solemnly.

"Don't think. I don't want you to. Thinking is not a good idea in situations like this. What you must do is feel. Then you will be certain to say yes. After all, I did not go to the trouble of locking that door for nothing."

"You? You did that?"

"I'm afraid so," he said. "You see before you a desperate man." He smiled at her. "Of course, I could have escaped out the window if I changed my mind—but I won't."

Regina unlocked the door, then turned and smiled tenderly at him. "I see before me an arrogant man, my lord."

"I do not think so." Lord Audlin rose, took several eager steps toward her, and stretched out his arms. She backed away.

He kept on coming. Still with her eyes on him, she used the side of her foot to push a squat little stool into his path.

Intent only upon catching his quarry, the earl did not see it. He tripped over it and started to fall. Before he reached the carpet, however, he grabbed hold of Regina. Down she went with him, landing atop him.

Deftly the earl rolled over, until she was pinned beneath his body. "Let me up," Regina said breathlessly.

"Certainly," said the earl. He did not do so, however. Instead he put his mouth to hers and kissed her. Then he kissed her some more. After that he kissed her a great deal more.

Finally Regina, her lips red and tingling from her beloved's kisses, pushed him away. "Enough," she said.

The earl looked crestfallen. "Didn't you like that?" he asked.

"I did. I liked it very well. In truth, of the three falls we've taken—down the hill, into the water, and now this—I believe that I like this best."

"So do I," said the Earl of Audlin, before kissing her again. "So do I."

Behind them, the door opened. Lady Sanding and Mr. Hammond stood without, along with Sally and Mr. James. Lady Sanding smiled, shut the door, and pulled Mr. Hammond away from the scene. "That little minx," she said. "She did it all herself."

"Did what?" asked Mr. Hammond. "Let go of me, Lucy. I've got to go in there."

"Indeed, you don't," she said, "and please lower your voice. Everything is all right now. You can trust me."

National Bestselling Author
PAMELA MORSI

"I've read all her books and loved every word."
—Jude Deveraux

WILD OATS

The last person Cora Briggs expects to see at her door is a fine gentleman like Jedwin Sparrow. After all, her more "respectable" neighbors in Dead Dog, Oklahoma, won't have much to do with a divorcee. She's even more surprised when Jed tells her he's just looking to sow a few wild oats! But instead of getting angry, Cora decides to get even, and makes Jed a little proposition of her own...one that's sure to cause a stir in town—and starts an unexpected commotion in her heart as well.

___0-515-11185-6/$4.99 (On sale September 1993)

GARTERS

Miss Esme Crabb knows sweet talk won't put food on the table—so she's bent on finding a sensible man to marry. Cleavis Rhy seems like a smart choice...so amidst the cracker barrels and jam jars in his general store, Esme makes her move. She doesn't realize that daring to set her sights on someone like Cleavis Rhy will turn the town—and her heart—upside down.

___0-515-10895-2/$4.99